THE TURNABOUT YEAR

1917 was the year the United States entered the great World
[...] rth Dakota,
[...] it would
[...] of some-
[...] before the
[...] ool. It was
[...] s, who had
[...] g, and that
[...] illage. She

[...] new baby,
[...] s, camping
[...] ed a part of
[...] ction could
[...] f she might
[...] with Father

[...] ales, North
[...] st began to
[...] and most

In this series:

The Turnabout Year

The Turnabout Year

by Lucy Johnston Sypher

ILLUSTRATED BY RAY ABEL

PUFFIN BOOKS

For All My Family
and
For All My Friends

PUFFIN BOOKS
Published by the Penguin Group
Viking Penguin, a division of Penguin Books USA Inc.,
375 Hudson Street, New York, New York 10014, U.S.A.
Penguin Books Ltd, 27 Wrights Lane, London W8 5TZ, England
Penguin Books Australia Ltd, Ringwood, Victoria, Australia
Penguin Books Canada Ltd, 2801 John Street, Markham, Ontario, Canada L3R 1B4
Penguin Books (N.Z.) Ltd, 182–190 Wairau Road, Auckland 10, New Zealand

Penguin Books Ltd, Registered Offices: Harmondsworth, Middlesex, England

First published in the United States of America by Atheneum, 1976
Published in Puffin Books, 1991
1 3 5 7 9 10 8 6 4 2
Copyright © Lucy Johnston Sypher, 1976
All rights reserved

Library of Congress Catalog Card Number: 91-52567
ISBN 0-14-034553-1

Printed in the United States of America
Set in Janson

Contents

The Turnabout Year

New Year's Eve

Outdoors, the last night of 1916 was dark and very cold, and the tiny village of Wales, North Dakota was deep in snow. But indoors, the Johnstons' living room was cozy and snug. The tall kerosene lamp on the center table shed a glow over the whole room, and through the isinglass windows of the stove doors shone the heaped red coals.

Lucy and her two best friends, Gwendolyn and Gwinyth Owen, sat close together, their chairs tilted back and their feet propped on the warm nickel rim of the base-burner stove. Nearby, Mother gently rocked in her favorite chair, humming to herself. Although Mother was well along in her forties, she was expecting a baby in a couple of months, and already she was as wide as her chair.

Father was reading beside the lamp. Suddenly he slapped down his magazine on the table. "Not a single piece of good news! The Allies are stuck in the trenches on the Western Front, and the Germans are sinking most of the ships on the ocean."

Lucy's brother, Amory, called cheerily from the kitchen. "How many poppers of popcorn for the rest of you? Jerry and I will want two apiece."

"Two full ones for each of you? Someday you'll pop!" Mother warned.

"Popcorn's mostly air, isn't it, Mr. Johnston?" asked Gwen.

"If it's only air, I'm getting stung. That last twenty-pound sack I got from Iowa cost a mint."

Mother turned toward him. "Harry, with a new baby coming and the war in Europe putting up all the prices here, should we still buy popcorn by the gunny sack?"

Amory answered her. "Baby or no baby, war or no war, I've used the last of it." They heard him rattle the hard corn into the long-handled popper and then scrape it to and fro across the stove-lids of the kitchen range. "I've melted the butter, too. What was in the butter crock seemed enough."

"Enough? That was almost a pound." Mother stopped rocking. "And these days I can't trade piano lessons for butter."

"There, there, Caroline," Father said. "We're short on cash, but we can still afford butter."

"And my recipe for popcorn is half corn and half melted butter." Amory came into the room, his arms around a huge kettle of popcorn, golden with butter. Amory was only one one year older than Lucy and not much larger, but he talked so much and he moved so fast that he seemed far bigger than he was. "Take some, everybody. That's Jerry at the back door." He plunked the kettle in Lucy's lap and ran to let Jerry Fischer in. As a special celebration for New Year's Eve, Gwen and Gwin and Jerry were staying overnight.

Jerry came in and politely spoke to the grown-ups. To the girls he said nothing. He was two years older than Amory, but not so old that he practised his politeness on girls.

"Funny that a year ago we didn't know each other," Gwen mumbled as they munched their popcorn.

"And a year from now we won't live in Wales," Gwin added. Lucy wished that Gwin hadn't mentioned it. She didn't like remembering that Methodist ministers and their families moved every year; for when the Owens left, she'd again be the only girl her age living in the village.

Then out on the road, a team of horses with jingling harness bells stopped in front of the house. After a man's loud WHOA! WHOA! other voices called, and soon people were on the front porch. At once, Father was at the door to let them in. When it was way below zero, he liked to open and close the double front doors himself. "Come in, come in," he boomed.

In trooped the two younger Owens, Guinevere and Edward. Behind them was Mrs. Sanderson, the village practical nurse, and her son, Stan. Amory let out a whoop. "Wahoo! Stan, can you stay the night too?"

"If your folks will let me. Ma's got to go out to nurse at Morgans' farm and Pa's not home. And look what I brought." He began to whisper as he pressed close to Amory and Jerry to show them something that Lucy couldn't see.

"The doctor's sleigh, isn't it?" Father asked.

"And is Doctor Carmer sober on New Year's Eve?" Mother asked.

"Yes, it's early so he's fine tonight. I was staying with the younger Owens, you know. Can you keep them until their folks come back from their Hannah church tomorrow? And is there space for Stan, too?"

"Of course, of course," Father assured her. "A house packed full of children—wonderful way to start the new year."

"Who's sick at Morgans'?" Mother pulled Mrs. Sanderson's scarf higher.

"That Canadian bride of Danny Morgan. Came only last week, and she's been out at that farm ever since. The doctor says it sounds like appendicitis."

They all knew that the nearest hospital was over a hundred miles away, but Mother asked anyway. "If it's an emergency, will he operate tonight at the farm?"

"Yes, if he has to, he'll do it on the kitchen table. Now I've got to go. I mustn't keep him waiting." Father opened the doors, Mrs. Sanderson hurried out, and Father slammed them quickly to shut out the bitter cold.

"Come on to the kitchen, Stan. We'll share our dishpan of popcorn." The four Owens went into the living room, and Lucy stayed a moment with the folks.

"Awful!" Mother said. "It's bad enough to marry a Morgan without getting appendicitis too."

"At least she chose Danny Morgan. Nowadays he mostly runs the farm, while his brother Mike and the old man buy and sell the whisky they smuggle across the Canadian border for their blind pig," said Father.

North Dakota had a law against selling any liquor, but many towns had illegal saloons, nicknamed "blind pigs." Because Wales was almost on the Canadian border, the Morgans easily brought in the cases of whisky that they sold in the one-room shanty behind the livery stable. Though many people called it a disgrace, no one had ever been able to close the blind pig.

"Well, any Morgan's a bad risk for a marriage," Mother said severely.

"Not their cousin, Luke Morgan. He's good, and fighting now in the Canadian army," Lucy contradicted her. She had once helped Luke and felt that he was her special friend.

"Better watch out, Caroline. Lucy's seen that Luke Morgan only once, but she's so stuck on him that someday she may marry a Morgan."

Mother looked so shocked that Father patted her shoulder and they went into the living room, Lucy with them. There Edward was yelling, "A dishpan for me too!" He pulled off his scarf and cap and coat and galoshes and leggings and dumped them in a heap in the middle of the floor, then ran to the kitchen. Gwen, without a word, began to pick up his things.

"I'm afraid, Mr. Johnston, you'll have a hard time with our Edward," Guinevere said, as she carefully removed her outdoor clothes and neatly piled them on the sofa.

"No, Guinevere, but he may have a hard time with me. Edward!" Father barked. "Come back here and pick up your things." Edward stopped yelling for popcorn. Gwen stopped picking up the heap of clothes. And Father called once more. "Edward Albert Christian Owen, no popcorn until these are picked up." Edward was named for the Prince of Wales, and Father used the full name only when he meant business. Within seconds, Edward was back in the living room, piled his clothes on top of Guinevere's, and smiled up at Father. "Splendid!" Father said. "Amory, give him a big bowlful."

When the popcorn was all gone, Father suggested, "Let's sing one song together before Mrs. Johnston has to go to bed. She's under doctor's orders to rest, you know."

So Mother went to the black upright piano, and Gwin stood beside her. Gwin had a beautiful soprano voice, but the songs she knew best were Sunday school songs, so she chose "Brighten the Corner Where You Are."

"That's a stupid song," Amory objected. "Let's sing 'Old Macdonald Had a Farm,' and we boys will drown you out with our turkeys and cows and—"

"And pigs!" shouted Gwin. "You boys eat like pigs, so—"

"No squabbles to end a year," Mother said wearily. "We'll sing 'Pack Up Your Troubles in Your Old Kit Bag, and Smile, Smile, Smile'."

"Isn't all that smiling a lot like 'Brighten the corner'?" Stan asked.

"No! It's a war song," Gwen corrected him. "The British soldiers sing it when they march up to fight in the trenches."

"Grown men march up to get killed singing 'Smile, Smile, Smile'? They must be crazy!" Jerry was contemptuous.

"Don't you call the British crazy," Guinevere said sharply. "We're Canadian and we're not crazy any more than—"

Mother stopped the argument by striking the opening chords. Gwin started "Pack up your troubles," and everyone belted out the song at the top of his lungs.

But by now it wasn't a cheerful song to Lucy, and she wished she was singing "Brighten the Corner."

When they'd finished the last *Smile, Smile, Smile,* Mother got up from her piano stool. "Now where will they all sleep?" she asked Father.

"I'll manage that, Caroline. Two cots and the sofa will make a regular boys' dormitory down here." After Mother had said good-night and gone up to bed, no one was in a hurry to move. The bedrooms had no heat, only registers in the floor to let some of the warm air from the stoves go upstairs. But in below-zero weather, every register was shut tight to keep the heat downstairs.

Father leaned back in his sloping Morris chair and stretched out his legs. "So that your mother can go to sleep, Lucy, can you think of something quiet? How about trading resolutions for the new year?"

"Never! If resolutions aren't secret, you get reminded all year about what you resolved to do."

"And they're kid stuff," Amory sneered. "I'm not making any."

Father looked disgusted. Then he had a new idea. "How about prophecies for the New Year? Each make one, and a year from now we'll see who was the best prophet. You begin, Gwen. What's your prophecy for 1917?"

Gwen never spoke hastily, so for a moment she sat quiet. Then she said, "I prophesy a year of changes, like our moving to another church for Papa."

"Mightn't you stay one more year so we could have the eighth grade together?" Lucy suggested. Gwen didn't answer.

Guinevere spoke up. She wasn't at all sad about moving. Ever since she had visited last summer in eastern Canada, she had talked about living in a city instead of a village like Wales. "I prophesy we'll move back to a city in Canada, and we'll have trees and streetcars and a big church and a big city school."

Father frowned. "Villages with small churches and schools are nice too, Guinevere." He didn't want to live anywhere else.

But often now Lucy thought about living in a city. She dreamed of living in a city house with electric lights and a bathroom, of walking on concrete sidewalks past blocks and blocks of houses, of going to a big, brick school with city girls and city boys. In the Wales school she'd been with the same people since the first grade. She longed for a change.

"Can I have my turn next?" Gwin asked. "I prophesy the war will end in 1917. And of course the Allies will win, and we'll kill the German Kaiser and all his German generals and his admirals and his U-boat captains and his—"

"Wait a minute, Gwin. You've killed enough for one young girl," Father interrupted. "And I fear the war can't end unless America goes in."

"Let me have that for my prophecy," Jerry said. Then very slowly he repeated. "In 1917 America will go to war." It sounded so solemn that no one said anything until Stan broke the silence.

"If we do go to war, my pa says he'll go work on a ship like he used to. He's promised to work on the Dunns' farm until winter, and then we'll go."

"Whatever will Wales do without your mother?" Lucy asked. "But she'll be here when we have our baby. I prophesy a baby girl."

"A baby boy," Amory contradicted her. "You're going to get another brother."

"I've got you, and one brother's plenty!" Lucy was emphatic.

"I'm plenty in our family, aren't I?" boasted Edward. "And I prophesy I'm going to wear boots to school, like the big boys."

"But Edward dear, that's not a prophecy. You know your new boots are in a box on the shelf, ready to wear," Gwen reminded him.

"That's why I said it. My prophecy is already true, so I've won," Edward crowed.

"I can prophesy something already planned too," Amory said. "I'm finishing all the high school there is here, so next fall I've got to go away to that military school in Minnesota, Pillsbury Academy."

Jerry echoed him. "I've got to go to the county high school in Langdon, but that's not really away, is it?"

"Away to school!" Gwin half sang the words. "Lucy you'll be stuck here in Wales for three more years—eighth grade and two years of high school. And we'll be gone and the boys will be gone and don't you wish you could go away too?"

"It would be nice," was all that Lucy said. Secretly she envied all of them, but she knew she hadn't a chance of going away too. The only time she'd mentioned it, Father had said, "One away at school is all we can afford." And Mother had said, "Why, Lucy, you won't be twelve until August. You're still a child."

Gwen summed up all the prophecies. "Everything's going to change. Nothing will be the same, will it, Mr. Johnston? If America goes to war, the whole country will be different, and Wales will be different, and we'll be different too."

"That's right, Gwen. If your prophecies come true, 1917 will be a turnabout year."

"What's a turnabout year?" asked Guinevere.

"It's just what we've said—a year when everything and everybody changes, and changes a whole lot. If it's a regular turnabout from the way things were before, then it's a turnabout year."

He stood up. "So much for the year ahead of us. Now to bed for the last hours of 1916. You three biggest girls will sleep in Lucy's double bed, and Guinevere and Edward can fit in Amory's bed."

"I'll sleep down here," Edward stated. "Amory can sleep with Guinevere."

"Sleep with Guinevere!" Amory was horrified.

"With eight children in this house tonight, I'm making the decisions." Father spoke sharply. "All set? You upstairs people take off your shoes and go quietly. You boys help me put up the cots. Good night until next year!"

Up into the frosty bedrooms the four Owens and Lucy tiptoed, and soon they were packed into the beds, under three blankets and a thick quilt of down. The cotton flannel sheets were fuzzy and soft, and the three girls warmed each other in Lucy's wide bed.

After a while the downstairs was quiet, and Father came up the creaky wooden stairs, went into the front bedroom and shut the door. Everything was silent.

"It's a good way to start the new year, with a best friend on each side of me," Lucy said to herself. "But it'll be a turnabout year for everybody but me. They'll go away and they'll change, and I'll stay the same. I wish my prophecy had been to go away too, but I'd have to keep it secret, like a dream." And in no time she was sound asleep and dreaming.

BANG! BANG! BANG! In a jiffy the girls were awake. Edward screamed. And Guinevere raced into Lucy's room, whimpering, "The war's begun." Edward followed her and jumped into the big bed, smack onto Lucy's stomach.

"Quit it! Get off me!" Lucy shoved him over onto Gwen.

"What's going on?" yelled Father, running past their room and down the stairs, leaving open the door at the bottom.

"You children all right?" Mother called over Edward's howls.

"Somebody shot a gun outside," Gwin shouted back, as she knelt at the window and scraped away the coating of frost.

Mother came heavily into the room. Downstairs there was a great slamming of doors, and then Father's loudest voice. "Stan's father may have put those cartridges in a box labelled 'blanks,' but you've shot holes in the porch ceiling. You could have killed someone!"

"Who's killed? Is anyone killed?" Mother moved to the head of the stairs. "I knew that boy shouldn't get a rifle for Christmas."

Father paid no attention. "Give me that gun," he roared. "What in the mischief are you shooting it now for?"

To answer him, the two church bells and the school bell began to ring, and from Main Street came a cannonade of firecrackers and gunshots. At once, everyone upstairs and downstairs shouted, "Happy New Year!" and Amory's "HAPPY NEW YEAR!" was the loudest of all.

The Igloo

THE NEXT MORNING at a late breakfast, the kitchen stool and all the straight chairs were pulled up to the dining room table so that the four Owens and Stan and Jerry and the four Johnstons could eat together. Edward began complaining immediately. "This stool's just like a high chair. I don't want to sit on it."

"You don't have to sit with us, but only people at the table get breakfast," Father said calmly. Edward scowled, but he sat on the stool. To pacify him, Gwen quickly passed him her plate of scrambled eggs and bacon, Gwin handed him a thick slice of buttered toast, and Guinevere put a heaping spoonful of strawberry jam on the toast.

Amory watched the Owens. "Wish I had sisters like that. Lucy never gives me anything but her oatmeal."

"Perhaps if you sat on a high stool—" Mother began jokingly.

"Let's put him on the stool—let's!" Stan slid off his chair and grabbed Amory. Jerry caught Amory by the arm, and Lucy whisked away Amory's plate and put it in front of Edward's stool. "Move off, Edward. Amory's going to sit there." For once, Lucy felt she had allies in defeating Amory.

But the moment she got into the act, the boys came together as a solid front against her. Stan recaptured Amory's plate, Jerry let go of Amory's arms, and Amory had the last word, as always. To Father he said, "Lucy didn't listen to the blessing you read this morning. It was about being mindful of the needs of others, but when it comes to my needs, she—"

Mother interrupted. "Let's not have this a year of disagreements."

"Especially about prayers," Guinevere said primly.

"Much better to talk about the prophecies I hear you made last night. Every one is different, I suppose?"

"Mine that I made after I went to bed is even more different. It's secret," Lucy said.

At once, Jerry objected. "If you keep it secret, you can just say at the end of the year about any old thing, 'That's my secret prophecy come true.'"

"I'll write it down and have my father seal it in the bank vault for the year. Then I can't change it."

"How come you're so bright today? I never would have thought of that," Amory said with respect.

"If I lock it up for you, what will the bank examiner say about my handling secret prophecies?" Father teased. "Mind you make it brief so I can hide it."

Lucy went to his desk in the corner of the dining room, and standing with her back to the others, she printed in ink on a sheet of his insurance company stationery:

THIS YEAR I'LL GO AWAY
TO A BIG CITY SCHOOL.

The whole prophecy was in ten words, exactly like a telegram.

She folded the paper, slipped it in an envelope, and licked the flap. "Label it, Lucy," Father told her. "I don't want anyone opening it by mistake down at the bank." So Lucy printed on the outside: LUCY JOHNSTON'S PRIVATE PROPERTY.

None of this took long, and everyone had been silent, watching her.

"I'll bet it's for something silly, like wishing her hair would turn curly this year," Amory began.

"What all of you need is fresh air and exercise to use up your steam," Father said. "You boys clear the table and tend to the dishes. You girls make the beds and pick up some of the clutter. Then out you all go."

"The snow's like concrete, I bet. Let's slide on your Flexible Flyer, Amory," Stan suggested.

"I thought you boys might build an igloo today." Father began to plan. "I've got instructions in that book on Eskimos."

"What about us girls doing it, too?" Lucy asked. "I've read that Eskimo wives work on the igloos."

"They sure do," Amory agreed. "The women do all the heavy work that doesn't take brains, and the men do what takes skill. That's why they have a couple of wives."

The three Owen girls looked disapproving of this oversupply of wives for one family. "Do you think that's very moral, Mr. Johnston?" asked Gwin.

"Hmmmmmmm," said Father thoughtfully. "Remember they stay alive where we'd die in less than twenty-four hours. But don't worry, Gwin. We're only building an igloo in a Wales ditch."

The boys were outdoors first, and by the time the girls came out, there was already a deep pit in the snow-filled ditch in front of the house. The snow, cut in cubes as large as they could handle, was piled on one side. "Your turn now," the boys yelled. "We're going in by the stove to thaw our hands."

The girls found it cold work, but they followed Father's orders, and one by one, they cut and lifted big chunks of snow on a pair of shovels, held close together.

Before long, a heavy team, pulling a wagon box set on runners, drove up and stopped. Mr. Schneider was driving in from his farm. They all knew him, but today he was so wrapped up in his sheepskin jacket and ear-flapped cap and woolen scarf that there was nothing to recognize until he pushed down the scarf and called out, "Happy New Year!" Then from the wagon box behind Mr. Schneider came loud echoes. "Happy New Year!" Father went toward the sleigh, and out from under the old buffalo robe jumped Peter and Franz, the two Schneider boys, about the ages of Amory and Lucy.

"Those boys look frozen stiff. Let them thaw here at our house and pick them up on your way home," Father suggested.

"Peter's going to stay in town with his uncle. I've got to locate the druggist to get a prescription filled—both girls sick with sharp stomach pains." While Mr. Schneider talked, the two boys climbed out the back of the wagon box, and Peter sprinted around and climbed up to the seat beside his father.

Franz stood undecided. He was a little younger than Peter and seemed always in the shadow of his big brother. Now he came to the snow pit, pushed up the visor of his winter cap and slowly looked around at the piles of snow slabs. "What's it for?" he asked.

"It's an igloo, and the boys have left us to do all the work," Lucy explained.

"That's why the Eskimos have so many wives. Did you know that, Franz?" Guinevere asked him seriously.

Mr. Schneider laughed. "Don't get yourself a wife for the new year, Franz. I'll be back before long." He shook the reins, the harness bells rang, the two horses snorted great puffs of vapor, and the box sleigh went toward Main Street.

"Go on in by the stove, Franz," Father encouraged him. And Franz finally did go indoors.

"He's the quietest boy in my room at school," Gwin told Father. "He's in the fifth grade like me, but nobody calls me the quietest girl," Gwin confessed.

"Bright boy, but he's shy. I have an older brother—Lucy's uncle in Langdon—so I understand. The second in line always feels second," Father said.

Soon the front door opened and out raced the four who were the first boys in their families—Amory and Jerry and Stan, and Edward, behind them, wailing, "Wait for me! Wait for me!" Franz was the last one out. Lucy was glad that when her baby sister was born, she'd still be the oldest girl, the big sister.

Now began the building of the igloo. Father supervised, as the boys and girls together upended the chunks of snow around the pit, leaving a low door in front. The roof was a problem. "I know you'd like a rounded top of snow, but only the Eskimos can make that," Father said. "We'll use old boards, spread snow thickly, and pour on well water tonight. By tomorrow you'll have a roof of ice with a wooden underpinning."

When the old planks were placed and everyone was tossing snow on them, they heard sleigh bells again, this time the lighter tinkling bells on a fast-stepping horse. They leaned on their shovels to watch a red cutter sleigh come swiftly along the road and stop beside them.

Everyone knew Tim Hoffer, who was driving, and Miss Baxter, the primary room teacher, and Tim's sister, Mary, home for the holidays from Mayville Teachers' College. "Happy New Year!" they called, and at the same moment the igloo builders chorused their "Happy New Year!"

Tim immediately began to joke. "I hear your family's growing, Mr. Johnston. Building an addition?"

"Sure are," Amory answered. "Might be triplets."

"Or quadruplets for a sideshow," squealed Gwin.

Then she looked at Father's face and saw he didn't think that very funny, so she sidled over behind Gwen.

"One baby's enough for now," Miss Baxter said. Lucy remembered how pale and scared she had been when she first came to teach last September, and now she was rosy-cheeked and smiling.

Then Mary called, "Lucy, do you mind coming to get these books I borrowed? We're so wedged into this seat that if I get out, I can't possibly squeeze in again."

Lucy ran to the road, reached up for the books, and as she looked up, she saw that Mary also was more beautiful than she'd been before she went away to school. "She's a grown-up now," Lucy said to herself. "She's been away."

"When do you go back, Mary?" Father called.

"In ten days. I have to practise teach for six months."

Then Tim shook the reins, they all waved, and the horse trotted off, pulling the red sleigh over the snow.

"Like a Christmas card, isn't it?" Gwen said, as they watched them go.

"Until we pour on the water tonight, the igloo's done," Father said. "When you drive by next time, Franz, stop by for a little whale meat and blubber." Then Father looked closely at Franz. He was leaning against the front gate, half bent over, his face twisted with pain.

"What's the matter, Franz?"

"Cramps, I guess, like the kids at home. It really hurts."

"Here's your father, but you'd better come inside the house."

From the wagon box sleigh, Mr. Schneider called, "Hop in, Franz, and cover up." Father explained that Franz had been fine until a few minutes ago. "Must be what the others have," Franz's father said. "I've got the medicine for it."

"We'd be glad to have him stay here."

"No, if it's catching, he might spread it to your kids."

"The pain's not so bad now," Franz said as he slowly climbed in and Father tucked the fur robe around him. Then Father stepped back, and they were off.

"I hope I don't get that germ," Amory said. "That was sure a real pain he had, wasn't it?"

Father said nothing, only stood looking after the disappearing sleigh. Mrs. Owen soon phoned that she and Mr. Owen were home, so the girls left, after everyone had taken a turn crawling in and out of the igloo.

"Sometime soon we'll have a Boy Scout meeting here," Father said, but the boys barely listened.

"Race you to your house." Amory challenged Jerry, and the three boys were off at top speed along the frozen path through the yard, Amory as usual in the lead, though he had the shortest legs.

The Detective
and His Driver

WHEN EVERYONE else had gone, Lucy and Father worked together on the igloo walls, smoothing the rough blocks of snow with the edges of the shovels. Lately she had seldom talked with Father alone, and now she wanted to ask him for something. So she moved close beside him.

"Father, did you see last night that everyone else is going away? I'll be stuck here all alone for three more years. Can't I go away to school in the fall?"

"We can barely afford Amory's tuition, and he has to go. Three years isn't all that long. You'll have us, plus the baby, so you won't be alone, my dear."

"But after the Owens leave, my life in Wales will be very boring," Lucy complained.

"Boring? Fiddlesticks! Life in Wales is never boring.

Where else in the USA could you have an igloo? Now let's check the inside. You go first."

When Lucy crawled in on her hands and knees, the cold went right through her galoshes and the toes of her shoes, through the knees of her black stockings and her long underwear, and through her snow-crusted mittens. Her woolen dress, her thick sweater, even her winter coat were no use at all. For a moment she sat on the icy floor, shivering. But she couldn't get out until Father had crawled in after her.

Immediately he began to praise his igloo. "Isn't it a beauty? And all handmade."

At the risk of freezing, Lucy decided this was a good moment to ask for another favor. "If I have to wait for three years to go away, can't you take me on a trip? More than anybody, I want to travel and see new places." Father opened his mouth, and Lucy knew what he was going to say, so she barged ahead.

"You're right that we had an auto trip last summer, but I want a train trip with a night on a Pullman car. And don't tell me I was on a Pullman when I was four years old and I shut the end of my finger in a steel Pullman door. All I can remember is a doctor sewing it on again. And it's crushed and it's crooked. That's not travel!"

"Seemed like a long trip to your mother and me," Father teased. "And expensive too. We even had to pay that doctor on the train for his crooked sewing." Then he spoke seriously. "It's true that the more trips you make, the more ready you'll be when it's finally time to leave home. But mind what I say—you've a lot of growing up to do. You need a regular turnabout from a child to a grown girl."

Father closed his mouth and set his jaw, and Lucy

saw that he was done talking. So she crept out, just as a sleigh with two men pulled up beside the ditch. The man beside the driver jumped out and came to the igloo. He was a stranger to Lucy, and he had to be a city man because he wore a long, black, fur-lined coat and a fur cap like Dr. Carmer's.

"Is this where Mr. Johnston lives?" the stranger asked.

"Yes, sir, this is his house," Lucy replied.

The man didn't look toward the house, only stared at the igloo. There, crawling out, was Father in his torn sheepskin jacket with his cap pulled over his eyes. "GRRRRR!" Father growled in his loudest voice. "GRRRRR!" he growled again. "Beware! Beware! I'm a polar bear!"

Then he pushed up his cap and saw the city man's startled look. Father stood up and grinned. "Want to see the inside of our igloo?"

The man never cracked a smile. "I was told that Mr. Johnston was the best educated man in Wales and could help me, but perhaps—"

"Perhaps you hadn't expected to meet a bear?" Father joked.

"Are you or aren't you Mr. Johnston? And is this where you live?" the stranger asked severely.

"Yes, I'm Mr. Johnston, and only occasionally am I a polar bear living in an igloo." Father now became all seriousness. "What can I do for you?"

"I want to talk with you alone for a few minutes. Here's who I am." He pulled out a flat leather case, opened it, and held it out to Father.

"The burglar alarm at the bank is set for the long weekend," Father explained, "so we'll have to talk here at the house." Then seeing the stranger hesitate, Father

said, "The house we live in most of the time, not this winter cottage." Lucy could tell by his expression that he thought the stranger was a nitwit, in spite of his city clothes.

"I'll have my driver take the rig to the livery stable. He's new to me, but he's from just across the border, and he says he's been in Wales before." At the sleigh as the two men talked for a moment, it was the driver who interested Lucy. He wore one of the face-covering knitted winter helmets that she'd seen only in pictures of the troops on the Western Front. She moved closer and watched the city man take out change to hand to the driver, who pulled off his glove to take the money.

As the coins clinked into the driver's palm, she clearly saw his index finger. It was crooked and crushed at the end, exactly like her own. She stared longer than was polite, but when she looked at his face to smile an apology, two brown eyes were all she saw. All the rest was hidden in the masklike khaki helmet.

Then the sleigh started off, the city man called, "See you soon at the livery stable," and Father led the way into the house.

"Lucy, your mother's resting upstairs, I presume. Tell her there's someone here who wants to talk privately. You stay upstairs too until you hear the front door shut."

Closing the stairway door, Lucy heard Father say, "Any child hears more than you think. 'Little pitchers have big ears,' but up there she can't hear anything."

Lucy hated being called a child or a little pitcher, so alone on the dark stairs she safely made a face and stuck out her tongue. Then she went to Mother's bedroom. "Is it a farmer we know?" Mother asked.

"No, but he must be important. He dresses like Dr. Carmer and he carries his name in his pocket like a detective. He speaks Canadian, too."

"Well, Mrs. Sherlock Holmes, you noticed a lot in a short time, but there's no such language as Canadian."

"When Father said he couldn't take him to the bank, he said, 'Eye-ther the bank or the house will do.' Dr. and Mrs. Carmer and the Owens say 'eye-ther.' That's not American."

"Detective or not, he's not here to arrest eye-ther of us, so I'm going back to sleep," and Mother turned over.

Lucy went to her own room, first pulling from Amory's bookcase his copy of *Tom Swift, The Detective*. She sat on her bed, wrapped the down quilt around her, and began to read. By the fourth page she had been introduced to two murdered bodies and a policeman so baffled that only Tom Swift could possibly solve the case. Could Wales have had a murder last night? Or was the crime committed in Canada and the killer now in Wales?

Her room was directly over the dining room, where Father talked with farmers on business. If she could get to the hot-air register without stepping on the two squeaky boards, she might truly be a little pitcher and hear about the crime before anyone else in the village. Holding the quilt around her, she soundlessly tiptoed toward the register. The first squeaky board was no problem, but she wasn't sure about the next one. So she edged along slowly until, almost at the register, she grew careless and put her foot down firmly on the cracked board. *SQUEAK!*

She froze and listened. Father's voice went on rumbling in the room below, and when she leaned over the register, she saw why his words did not come through clearly. The register was shut tight. How could she click open that old iron register so silently that the men wouldn't hear her?

Deftly she inserted a corner of the soft eiderdown quilt where the lever opened the metal fins. Then she gradually shifted the lever from SHUT to OPEN. The click was so deadened that she barely heard it herself. Now she could hear Father's actual words. "You say you're from the East and new out here, so I'll tell you that whisky is regularly smuggled across the border to sell in Wales and all over Dakota. Now when you talk of a spy—"

The man spoke in a faint mumble that Lucy couldn't hear.

"You're right about their being German-Americans, but I know all the farmers around for miles—honest, hard workers, every one of them," Father said. "I'm sure Wales has no spy."

There was another soft murmur and then Father's voice. "Yes, if I hear anything, I'll report it. Let me help you on with your coat. Quickest way to Main Street is along our back walk. You'll probably find your driver in high spirits. The illegal whisky is sold right behind the livery stable. Have a Happy New Year!"

Lucy heard the door slam before Father called, "You can come down now." She softly slid the register lever to SHUT, spread her quilt across the bed, and sauntered downstairs.

Mother followed her. "Who was it, Harry?"

"A Canadian detective, but he's from the East and he's a babe in arms when it comes to a small prairie village like Wales. He sent his driver to the livery stable, and I'll bet every lounger on Main Street knows or guesses everything by now."

"Yes, even Lucy spotted the man as a detective." Mother laughed. "Lucy, did you ever think you might grow up to be a detective?"

"Grow up to be one?" Lucy said to herself. "I've just been one!" Aloud she said nothing at all, but to herself she vowed she'd not only be the first to hear about the spy but she'd be the one to catch him. That would prove she wasn't still a child.

Because it was New Year's Day, dinner was in mid-afternoon. The three of them had just sat down when Amory came in with a shout. "Would you believe it? A detective from Canada was right here in Wales a couple of hours ago and his driver says they're looking for a German spy."

"We know about that already," Father said. "Wash your hands and come eat."

"And I talked to the detective, too," Lucy bragged.

"You talked to him?" Amory came into the dining room, dripping soapy water.

"Use the towel," Mother said gently, but firmly.

Amory backed toward the kitchen and reached behind him to dry his hands on the roller towel hanging on the door. "Where did you see him? What did he want to talk to you for?"

"Actually, the man paid more attention to Lucy at first than he did to me." Father chuckled. "When he arrived, I was crawling out of the igloo, playing I was a polar bear and growling fiercely."

"Harry, you weren't!"

"Nothing illegal about a man playing polar bear, is there? But I'll admit Lucy did impress him more than I did, until I stopped growling."

"How did you find out, Amory?" Without a register, he knew it all.

"The driver went through the livery stable to the blind pig behind it for a drink, didn't he?" Father guessed.

"Yup, and afterwards we boys heard George Henderson in the livery stable telling what the driver said. He said . . . well, all he said was that someone in Wales is a German spy."

"Amory Johnston, don't you go near that blind pig and don't hang around the livery stable or the pool hall or . . ." Mother launched a series of don'ts, but she forgot the rest and asked Father, "A spy? In Wales? That's not possible, is it?"

Amory answered her. "America's not at war yet, so someone could sneak information across the border and send it to Germany from the USA, couldn't he? And around here almost everybody is German and wants Germany to beat the Allies, too. So one of them might be a—"

Father cut him off. "Both you children listen to me." He spoke in his deepest bass voice. "Close as we are to the Canadian border, someone could be a go-between for a spy, for a good sum of money too. But soon we'll be at war, and then there will be false rumors about all German-Americans, even here in our village. I won't have you two listening to any such unfair gossip. Is that clear?"

Amory and Lucy nodded, but since they heard everything in the village, how could they not hear rumors?

Lucy ventured one question. "Just on the chance there is a spy in Wales, shouldn't we hunt for him?" She watched Father's face, and then added, "I mean if we did it very quietly and didn't spread any rumors or bother anybody?"

"Maybe there's a big cash reward." Amory took up the idea. "I could use a hundred dollars extra when I go away and—"

"No cash offered, Amory, and probably no spy would stay here anyway, now that the news has spread through the stable and the blind pig." Father looked cross. "That driver is either a first-class dummy or he's a crook himself and a lot brighter than that numbskull detective. Now there's a real idiot!"

"Possibly he has the same opinion of a grown man pretending he's a polar bear," Mother teased. Father looked sheepish, so she changed the subject. "Mrs. Sanderson phoned from Morgans' farm. The doctor did have to operate last night, and he expects the girl to live, but she's still very, very sick."

The Spy Hunt

NEW YEAR'S NIGHT Lucy sat indoors with Mother, learning to cross-stitch on a baby's blanket, while Amory and Father doused the igloo with pails of water from the backyard pump. "I'm glad you stayed in with me," Mother told her. "It's good for a father and son to work together."

Mother had no sooner said the words, than Amory rushed in, dripping icy water and moaning loudly, "I'm freezing! He nearly drowned me!"

Father was right behind him, carrying an empty pail. "I'd no idea that you were on the other side of the igloo, Amory. I thought you'd gone back to the well."

Amory stood close to the stove, pulling off his plaid mackinaw and then the rest of his wet clothes. "Why, Harry, in below-zero weather that boy is soaked to the skin." Mother spoke reprovingly. "I believe that igloo changes your character."

"Do you think I'll get pneumonia?" Amory asked in a doleful voice, as he stood shivering in his wet underwear.

Though Father was probably cross with himself for the accident, he now sounded cross with Amory. "Of course you won't get sick. North Dakota is almost germless. Our air's too pure and our winter's too cold. You get dry and stay by the stove. I'll finish the job." He banged out of the house, and Mother sent Lucy upstairs for Amory's flannel pajamas and two blankets to put around him.

When Father came in, Amory was reading by the stove in his warm wrappings. Mother said nothing about water or igloos, and certainly nothing about a father and son working happily together. Lucy kept quiet, her nose buried in *Tom Swift, The Detective*.

The day after New Year's, the Owen girls came over for a meeting of the girls' club, which Amory had named the Stone Age Girls because in the summer they met in the little stone house.

"Let's meet in the igloo," Lucy suggested, as she piled on her heavy clothes to go out with them. After all four of them crawled in and sat in a circle in the house of snow and ice, Lucy began to talk. "There's a spy right here in Wales. After you went home yesterday, a Canadian detective was in our house and told my father. Why don't we hunt for the spy, all of us? He's a German spy, passing messages to the enemy. Can't you imagine how famous our club would be if we discovered him? Can't you see how important we'd be?" As Lucy talked, her visions of greatness spread out and out. Probably there would be a reward of heaps of money, and maybe even medals, and perhaps they'd be called to Winnipeg to be thanked by a general or even by a whole regiment with a brass band playing and flags flying.

"A Wales spy? That is in-cred-ible!" Guinevere had recently learned the word and loved it.

"Wales could have a spy just as easily as Winnipeg," Gwen said. "Lucy, you know Wales best. Where do we begin?"

"We've got to make a list of all the Germans we know," Gwin said, while Lucy was still thinking. "Willie Baumgarten's mother is very German and mixes up German and English when she talks. And right in your block, Lucy, Hilda Dickerman's mother is German as German can be."

"Make a list of all the Germans? Are you crazy?" Lucy asked. "Most of the families around here are German. They can't all be spies. Besides, Mrs. Dickerman's going to have a baby in the spring. She doesn't have time to be a spy."

"Family people wouldn't do that sort of thing anyway," Gwen said. "More likely it's someone living alone. Then he could be very secret."

"How about the priest, Father Van Mert?" Gwin suggested. "He hasn't got a family, and couldn't Magic, his talking crow, learn messages and pass them on to another spy?"

Lucy settled that. "Father Van Mert is Holland Dutch and not German, and Magic is a crow and not a carrier pigeon. He's got a new housekeeper too, and she's German, but she talks so much that nobody'd hire her for a spy. She'd tell everything in five minutes. The priest told my father, 'That Mrs. Ludwig is driving me bats with her babbling,' or however a priest would say it," Lucy concluded.

"Mrs. Bortz lives alone and her two nephews were killed in the Kaiser's army, and—"

Lucy didn't let Gwin finish. "I like Mrs. Bortz, and she likes me, and I heard her say once that she's American now and not German any more."

"Old Mrs. Schnitzler lives alone, when she's not out at her son's farm," Gwen said.

"But winter's when she's at the farm. Anyway, she's got so much rheumatism and so little English that she couldn't carry messages or anything else." Lucy was definite.

"All right! All right! We'll skip the women and get on to the men who don't have families." Gwin sat thinking a moment and then exclaimed. "I've got it! Dennis Beaupray's back from Canada, and he lives alone in his shack."

"But Beaupray's a French name. He's not German, and ever since he froze his fingers off in a blizzard, he's got only stumps for hands. Who'd ask a man to carry messages when he can't carry anything at all?" Gwen sounded very superior.

Lucy spoke up quickly. "That leaves only the butcher, Ed Berman. He doesn't exactly live alone, but he has a room by himself at Mrs. Moors's hotel and he's German."

"And sometimes his shop is shut tight for two or three days," Guinevere said. "So what's he doing then?"

"When he's drunk too much whisky, he shuts up shop. That's all," Gwen told her.

"But how do we know?" Guinevere continued.

"Maybe spy messages are in those whisky bottles from Canada. Aren't messages sometimes put in bottles?"

"Those are bottles to float in the sea. Wales is a couple of thousand miles from any ocean," Lucy explained. "But I don't know. I just wonder. Ed Berman does have a lot of empty bottles. One time Amory brought home six of them with corks, and he was going to put homemade root beer in them. But when Mother heard where they came from, he had to take them right back to the trash heap behind the butcher shop. She almost had a fit."

"I think both our mama and our papa would have a fit if we collected whisky bottles," Gwen said, and they all giggled.

"Let's go inside the house." Guinivere stood up. "I'm frozen stiff. This igloo really isn't good for much, is it?"

"It was fun to build," Lucy answered.

"What's the good of building something if you can't use it?" Gwin asked. "Your father's funny, isn't he, Lucy?"

Not liking to hear her father called funny, Lucy countered with a criticism of Mr. Owen. "Your father makes model trains, so my father's igloo is just as good as that."

"Oh, no," Guinevere disagreed. "Papa's model trains come from England, and this igloo is just old North Dakota snow."

"I think maybe men never grow up," Gwen began. "Papa does like little trains, and Lucy's father makes a snow house, but our mothers don't play with dolls, do they? I wonder when it happens."

"When what happens?" Lucy asked.

"When the women grow up and the men don't."

"It hasn't happened yet to me. Amory's only one year older, and my folks think he's old enough to go away to school. But when I talk about going away, they say I'm not ready."

"It's not fair," Gwen agreed. "But we're freezing in this icebox." And the girls raced for the house. Mother met them at the door and asked them to go to Main Street on errands—crackers and tomato soup from Lowensteins' and sausages from the butcher shop.

"That is, if it's open, of course," Mother added, and the girls smirked at each other. They ran out the back shed and along the snowbank path to the back gate. The sun was already very low and crimson; and in the sharp cold, every footstep squeaked on the frozen snow. At Lowensteins' Lucy picked up the brown bag of groceries, and at the bank she collected the mail for Mother. Coming to the butcher shop, they peered in the storefront window before they entered.

Ed didn't say hello or joke as he sometimes did, only reached up to the big hooks in the ceiling and pulled down two loops of the hanging sausages. Then his wooden cuckoo clock whirred, the little door at the top opened, and the tiny yellow cuckoo bobbed out and chirped, "Cuckoo" four times. Immediately Ed was in a better humor.

"My clock's always right. You can trust the cuckoo."

"Can you trust it with secrets?" Lucy asked, giving Gwen a knowing look after she asked him.

"Of course I can." Ed winked at them. "Nobody, not even the clockmaker, knows what a cuckoo does, hiding in its little house."

"It doesn't call in German, but maybe in a secret code?" asked Gwin, watching the butcher's red face closely.

"Yah, yah. That's it." The butcher stroked his long red moustache. Then he surprised them with another joke. When it says one cuckoo, that means, 'I got you!' But when it says, 'Cuckoo, cuckoo,' listen! 'Not true! Not true!' " He laughed at his own joke.

"And three times?" Glinevere was staring at him intently.

"That's easy." Ed wrapped the sausages and handed them to Lucy. "Sometime you come by at three o'clock. Then it's 'No clue! No clue! No clue!' "

By now Ed was so tickled by his own story that when Gwen pleased him by asking, "And what does it say at four?" he went to the wall rack of square tin containers of cookies and handed each girl a round cookie topped with bright pink marshmallow and sprinkled with cocoanut. "Four cookies to say Happy New Year to the four of you!"

"That's the best code of all! My mother never makes cookies like these," Lucy told him.

Though it seemed ungrateful after the cookies to search for his whisky bottles, they did go around the block and come back behind his shop. The trash heap

was snow and ice and ashes. Not a single bottle there.

"But that clock," Guinevere said as they went toward home. "Wouldn't it be a good place to hide a scrap of paper?"

"It's Ed we have to watch, not his clock. And we're serious about this spy hunt," Lucy said. "Cookies and cuckoos are fun, but we've got to spy on the spy, and secretly too."

The next noon Amory had a throbbing toothache. The nearest dentist was in Langdon, twenty miles away. "You'll have to go down on the train this afternoon, Amory. Your Uncle Charlie can get you an appointment, and your Aunt Effie is always glad to have you cousins together," Father said.

"Can't I go too?" Lucy begged. "Cousin Gen and Cousin Kink are home from college and I—"

"Not this time," Father interrupted her. "That house barely holds the cousins, and when we add Amory for two nights . . ." Father stopped talking to Lucy and spoke to Amory. "Now that you're twelve, here's the money for a full-fare ticket and a little extra for spending."

Amory counted the money and forgot his toothache. "That's not enough. I really need more. There can be all kinds of emergencies when you travel."

"Travel!" Lucy said scornfully. "It's only twenty miles."

Amory went on arguing with Father. "When you think of all that could happen in twenty miles—the people who might try to steal my cash, the sandwiches I might have to buy if there's a candy vendor on the train, and then the cost of living in Langdon. Besides I think I got this toothache from that soaking you gave me New Year's night."

This was too much for Father. "Are you trying to blackmail me?" he sputtered. But he took out his little leather coin purse and handed Amory twenty-five cents more. "That's all you get. And are you sure you've still got that toothache, or is this a holiday jaunt?"

Amory shut his mouth and gripped his cheek again. Mother comforted him. "Poor boy, of course he's got a toothache, and the sooner he's on the way to the dentist, the better."

So very soon he was on the way, and Lucy was left at home. She didn't want a toothache, and going to Langdon on the Wales train wasn't her idea of travel, but she felt sorry for herself. "He goes away and I'm stuck at home; always it will be that way."

Stuff
and Nonsense

WITH AMORY GONE, Mother and Lucy spent hours that afternoon and the next day sewing baby clothes and talking, the kind of talk that Lucy called "woman-talk," all about babies and Mother's girlhood in the city and the lives of people she had known. One advantage to Mother's not giving music lessons this winter was this extra time spent with Lucy, and Lucy loved being treated like an equal.

Then on Thursday afternoon, Father phoned from the bank, asking Lucy to hurry down and put an important letter on the down-train for Grand Forks. "I can't leave the bank today, and this letter absolutely has to go. I promised," he said.

Lucy was running past the parsonage when the three Owen girls came out their gate, on the way to her house. "Come with me," Lucy said. "Got to catch the down-train. Very important letter to go." They raced together to the bank. Lucy picked up the letter, and Father repeated, "This must go, and hurry. I heard the train whistle a minute ago." So they charged along Main Street, almost colliding with farmers and their families as wrapped and padded and scarved against the cold as the girls were.

Before they got to the station platform, the train had pulled in and Tom Evans was handing up to the baggageman at the door of the baggage car two dirty gray canvas mail sacks. Lucy was just in time. She handed up her single envelope, saying, "Take this too. It's very important."

The baggageman reached down for it, and as he took it, Lucy saw part of the address—*Frau Berman* and *Germany*. "Ed Berman's letter, and if it goes from the bank, it must have money," she said to herself, as the baggageman shoved the door shut. Tom Evans waved a red flag to the engineer, and the train began chugging and then picking up speed for the long miles still to go.

Only one passenger had alighted, a short blond man wearing a black bowler hat, a black coat with the collar turned up to his ears, and light gray gloves. All four girls stood staring at him. He came toward them, set down his satchel, took from his pocket a pair of dark glasses, put them on, and then asked the girls one question. "Where's the butcher shop?" Only his German accent was so strong that it sounded like, "Vares da budger shob?"

For a moment the girls were speechless. Then Gwin, who had the quickest tongue, replied. "It's only a block or two from here. We'll take you."

"No! I find it myself." He picked up his satchel

and walked briskly along Main Street, the girls following a little way behind him.

"A bowler hat and gray gloves," murmured Gwin.

"And in Wales," marvelled Guinevere.

"What could be in that satchel? And those dark glasses—could he be another detective?" Gwen said, as the man outdistanced them and entered the butcher shop.

"My mother has to wear dark glasses when the sun glares on the snow, and she's no detective or a spy, either." Lucy paused. "And do you think a detective or a German spy would talk so German that everyone would notice him?"

"We notice him, but a lot of the Germans around here wouldn't," Gwen pointed out. By now the girls stood in a row, peering in the wide shop window, listening to the loud argument inside.

"Yah, yah, so I'm late," the stranger said rudely.

"I had to send the money today—a lot of money for me, and you've got money, too!" Ed shook his fist. "Somebody paid for those clothes, you city slicker!" he yelled. Then he looked at the window and saw the four girls, noses pressed to the pane.

In three long steps he was at the door, flung it open, and asked gruffly, "You girls want something?"

This time Lucy was the first to speak. "We just came by to hear your cuckoo say the hour."

"Then go on home, kids," he growled and slammed the door.

"Something's wrong with this whole thing," Gwen began as they walked away. "It's just too much like a spy story to be true. Ed pretending yesterday that his clock holds secrets and calls in code, and today that

German stranger comes and they quarrel about money."

"But, Gwen, he came on the train from Hannah, and we know most everybody in Hannah because of Papa's church there, and we never saw this man before, never." Then Gwin finished with a clincher. "He must have crossed the border from Canada and caught the train in Hannah."

"He could," Lucy agreed. "After Luke Morgan escaped from the county jail last summer, he just walked across the border at night."

"Do you think we should get the law on this?" Gwen asked. "Send an anonymous note to the sheriff, maybe?"

"To the sheriff?" Lucy was aghast. "He's the one that came here to shut up the blind pig and all he did was arrest Luke, a good Morgan. Let's not get any sheriff on this case!"

"Tomorrow let's buy something at the shop and see what's happened." Gwin went on planning. "We don't buy much, but doesn't your mother need bacon, perhaps?"

Later on, Mother's answer was no help. "Bacon? You know we've got a ten-pound slab hanging in the shed and more in the barn. What's got into you, Lucy— wanting to run errands? Must be a New Year's resolution. Now if you really want an errand, go to the cellar and hunt for a jar of currant jelly at the back of the shelf."

"A jar of jelly! I'm on a hunt for something more important than that," Lucy said to herself, as she went down to the dusky cellar.

Though there was no need for bacon, the girls

traipsed down to the bank on Friday afternoon for Mother's mail. As they turned onto Main Street, they slowed to pass the butcher shop, and just then the carved yellow cuckoo popped out of his little house and called, "Cuckoo! Cuckoo! Cuckoo!" The girls softly mimicked it, as they stared into the empty shop. "No clue! No clue! No clue!"

The wooden bird jerked backward, its tiny door clicked shut, and the shop was silent again.

On the way back from the bank, they couldn't resist pausing at Ed's window once more. This time they saw Ed Berman. He was standing with his back to them, pulling flat whisky bottles out of his deep coat pockets and putting them in a row on his counter. "He must have been to Canada," Lucy whispered. "And where's the man with gray gloves?"

"Ed must have left him in Canada," Gwin answered, under her breath.

"And maybe he brings back the messages in those bottles," Guinevere said right out loud. They *shhhhed* her and sneaked around to the trash heap. This time on top of the ice and ashes lay one flat brown bottle.

Gwin picked it up, pulled the cork and sniffed. "Something smelly in it, just a little at the bottom." She held it closer to her face and tilted it.

"Don't drink it!" Lucy yelled. "It might be poison!"

The back door of the shop opened, and Ed the butcher leaned against the doorway. He was very red in the face, his few spears of hair were mussed and every-which-way, and his eyes looked mean. "You kids! Get away from here!" he bellowed. The girls stood staring, too shocked to move. "You kids! I'll tell your folks!" he bellowed even louder. He lurched out the door.

Gwin dropped the bottle, and the four girls scooted at top speed along the path past the blind pig. Usually Guinevere complained that the other girls ran away from her, but this time she outraced them all.

When they reached the school steps, cold as the January day was, they sat down to catch their breath. Immediately, Amory appeared, lugging his suitcase. "I'll tell the folks, too," he echoed the butcher. "I saw you fooling around that trash heap, and worse than that, you ran on the path beside the blind pig."

"You must have come that way too," Lucy countered. "I could tattle on you."

Amory sat down on his suitcase, and he spoke seriously. "You girls shouldn't be there. The butcher gets drunk and the blind pig—well, that's not nice either. I don't want kids to say my sister hangs around there." This was a different Amory from the teasing one, so if he had stopped with that, Lucy would have listened. But he went on, almost sneeringly. "You're such babies, you need a guardian."

Lucy was furious. "We're not babies. I'll go where I like in this village," and she stuck out her tongue at him. "You mind your business, and we'll mind ours, Amory Johnston!"

He sprang up. "That does it. I was trying to keep you out of trouble. Now I'm going to tell Mother so she can lay down the law to you." And off he went, Lucy and the three girls chanting after him, "Tattletale! Tattletale! Hanging on a bull's tail!"

Lucy wanted to stop at the parsonage until she could think of an excuse for the butcher incident, but she was carrying mail that Mother would want. So she walked slowly toward the house and found Mother in the kitchen. She spoke the moment Lucy came in. "What's this Amory tells me about your hanging around the butcher shop and the blind pig?" Mother straightened her pince-nez glasses and waited for Lucy's reply.

"Amory tattled, didn't he? He goes that same path and lots more than I ever do."

Mother ignored the point. "What on earth were you girls doing at the butcher's trash heap? Right now —tell me. Your Father phoned he'd be home early for supper, and I don't want him upset."

Before Lucy could answer, Father banged the shed door. Mother gave Lucy a little shove. "Quick, dear, go set the table. He'll want supper."

Lucy scurried toward the dining room. She would have set ten tables happily to get out of this mess. Then Father opened the kitchen door and his first word was "Lucy!" Lucy stopped in her tracks. "Lucy!" he repeated even louder. "What's this the butcher tells me about you and the Owen girls?" Obviously Father was already upset.

"What does the butcher say?" Lucy asked innocently.

"You know very well what your father is talking about," Mother scolded.

"Ed called me in as I came by, and I admit he'd been drinking, but he says you girls have been annoying him, peeking in his window and rummaging in his trash." Father was getting up steam. "I won't have it! Ed's a good customer of mine, and besides, he's got troubles right now. He knows that pretty soon he can't send money to Germany to an old aunt, so he's just cleared his account and sent her all of it." By now, to Lucy's relief, Father was talking to Mother. "The old woman's son, Ed's cousin, wouldn't send her a red cent. Ed's a saint, that's what he is." Then he saw Lucy's expression of surprise. "Of course he drinks too much, but—and just what were you doing to him, Miss Lucy?" Father glared at her.

There was no way out. "We thought he might be a German spy," Lucy said in a voice as thin as a thread.

"A spy! Ed Berman a spy? Stuff and nonsense!" Father was boiling again. "And you ask why you aren't ready to go away to school! Don't you know that it's only in books that children catch the spy? Where's your common sense?" And Father went to the living room muttering, "I never heard of such stuff and nonsense, stuff and nonsense."

"Good thing school begins again on Monday. You say Miss Fothergill doesn't teach anything new, but at least you'll be busy," Mother said. This was the grown-up opinion that Lucy hated. How would Mother like to be shut up in that seventh-eighth grade room with fat old Fothergill all day long?

At supper, Amory brought news of the Langdon cousins. "Len's got the biggest chemistry set made. Uncle Charlies says Len may blow up the whole town, and I wish I had one like that." Amory knew it was only a wish, so he went right on. "Ed's begun singing lessons and goes around shouting, 'Fa, la, la.'" Amory imitated Ed at the top of his lungs. Mother handed him a cinnamon roll to stop his mouth.

"George is buying everybody's junk and getting rich." Amory talked through his sticky mouthful. "It's for the war, you know. Down in Langdon the war's a lot closer than it is in Wales. Cousin Gen's taking college courses about how to save food for the starving Europeans, and Cousin Kink might join the navy. And tin foil—everybody's collecting tin foil for—well, I'm not sure what for, but the Allies need it. How about my buying a dollar's worth of Hershey bars tomorrow and starting a roll of foil?"

"By the time you gobble twenty chocolate bars, you'll need the dentist again," Mother warned.

Amory dropped that scheme and jumped up. "Cousin Gen had war posters and gave me some. Wales hasn't had any like this." He ran upstairs to his suitcase and brought down a roll of stiff paper. He stood beside the table and unrolled them one at a time. The first one had a British officer in khaki uniform with a finger—an enormous finger—pointing out of the picture. Underneath it were the words, "Your country needs YOU!"

Lucy felt the finger pointing right at her, but it wasn't a frightening poster like the next one, with a beastlike soldier's green face under a monster helmet. One huge hand brandished a gun with a bayonet that dripped blood. At the bottom, on an ocean floor, lay heaps of drowned and dying people. "That's because German Huns are killing everybody with their guns and with their U-boats, too," Amory explained. "And the U-boats are why the Allies are starving, even the soldiers."

He went on with his poster display, showing a thin, tired soldier sitting in a mud trench and drinking from a dented tin cup. Above him were the big letters: FEED A FIGHTER, and below in smaller letters: *"Eat only what you need so that he may have enough."*

"Hmmmmm," said Father. "Amory, that would be a good slogan for you."

"But I do eat only what I need," Amory argued. "I just need a lot." He paused before he held up the last one. "It's a sad one." Lucy could see why he warned them. In the background blazed the fire of battle and the charred ruins of a town. In front of that sat a ragged child in wooden shoes, burying her face in the lap of an older girl, who was holding out her hand and pleading, "Have you room in your hearts for us?" and across the poster was printed: FUND FOR THE FATHERLESS CHILDREN OF FRANCE.

"I've had an appeal for that fund recently, but the letter didn't wring my heart the way this does," Father said. "Should we send some money, Caroline?"

"Oh, you must!" Lucy answered.

"You can arrange to have the money go to one child. Might do you children good to hear about a child that isn't as lucky as you."

Lest Father begin to preach, Lucy got up to bring in the pineapple upside-down cake. As she ate the gooey topping, she said to herself, "I am lucky. He needn't say it."

Miss Fothergill
Departs

WHEN LUCY told the girls the facts about the butcher, and that Father called him a saint, each girl said what Lucy had expected. Gwen reminded them that it had all seemed too much like a story to be true. Gwin began to plan a new campaign with a new list of German names, until Lucy warned her. "They're all my father's customers, and he says we mustn't even watch them." Then seeing Gwin's impatient look, Lucy added, "Anyway my father doesn't have spies for customers."

"Your father really is strange," Guinevere said. "My papa wouldn't call the butcher a saint—not in a thousand years. It's in-cred-ible!"

Gwen rallied to Lucy's father. "He didn't mean a saint in heaven, only in Wales, Guinevere." That satisfied everybody, and by now they were a little tired of the spy hunt. Vacation was almost over, and the old routine would begin again.

But by Monday the old routine was gone. "Mother!" Lucy yelled on Monday noon, as she came in from school. "Can you believe it—Miss Fothergill resigned, and she's leaving this afternoon. Today we had no teacher at all."

"No teacher? Your father won't like that. Last fall you spent so much time helping in Miss Baxter's primary room that he thinks you haven't learned a thing in the seventh grade."

"But I already knew what Miss Fothergill was teaching, except for some of the poetry she was always ramming down our throats."

"Cold out," said Father as he came in. And seeing Mother pour boiling water into the teapot, he added, "After a cup of that hot tea, I want to ask your advice, Lucy." He was always telling her to make decisions for herself, but he'd never before asked her to help him make a decision.

At the table Father explained. "The school board asked my advice this morning about getting a replacement for Miss Fothergill, and I—"

"You want me to advise the school board?" Lucy laughed. "You know what Guinevere always says, 'Incred-ible!'"

"They've wired the teachers' agencies, and there's not a single teacher available."

"So what then?" Lucy asked.

"Tell me, do you think Mary Hoffer could handle that bunch in your room—Mitch Garrity, for instance?"

Lucy thought a moment. Mitch was almost six feet

tall and old for the eighth grade, but he wouldn't be the problem. The seventh grade cutup, Cyril Oldham, would be Mary's problem. He was bright and funny and people liked him, but unless Mary could get him on her side, she'd never succeed.

Instead of trying to explain this, Lucy said, "I'd like to have Mary for my teacher. She'd be wonderful. Remember when we saw her country school last summer? All around the room she had drawings and bunches of flowers."

"Flowers in Dakota in January aren't likely," Mother said, "but she'd be good, Harry. She's lived in a family of brothers, really brought them up after her mother died."

Amory came to the table. "Your old Fothergill couldn't stand you any longer, Lucy. She'd rather spend her time with that drooling old bulldog, Mr. Guggums."

"But why is she leaving, Harry?" Mother asked.

Amory answered. "Old Guggums has a cold and the vet wouldn't come to see him, so she's taking that mutt away on the train today."

"Could that be so, Harry? The dog's so old that she must know he can't live much longer."

Since no one else in the family was a dog lover, Lucy spoke up. "Miss Fothergill hasn't got anybody else, and she said once that a dog is a person. And she's right. A dog isn't just a dog. It's more." Here Lucy's voice began to quaver as she thought of her own little terrier, Topsy, who had died in the fall.

Amory was busy eating and didn't see the tears gather in Lucy's eyes. "You and fatty Fothergill, both crazy as coots!" Then he looked up, saw Lucy's forlorn look, and before either Mother or Father could say anything, he comforted her. "That slobbering bulldog isn't a person, but your Topsy was. Sometimes I miss her too," and he gave Lucy his warmest smile. Since Amory seldom saw anything from Lucy's point of view, this was astounding. Lucy wiped her eyes and smiled back at him. "I was only saying how Fothergill felt. I don't feel that way about her old blob of a Mr. Guggums."

"Off the subject of dogs and back to a teacher," Father said. "The school board had me phone Mary this morning, and then I phoned Mayville and found they'll accept her teaching in Wales for her practise teaching semester, so she begins tomorrow morning."

"That's the way it always is. You knew all along that she'd be my teacher. You say I should make decisions, but you do as you please anyway." Lucy spoke grumpily.

"Now I've come to a decision right off the bat," Amory stated. "I'd like three pieces of that mince pie."

"My decision for you is only two pieces," Mother said.

"You see? I make up my mind, but you make the decisions. I'll never have a strong character that way."

"Oh, here, have a third piece. Where you put it all, I'll never know."

As Lucy was leaving for school again, she asked Mother's permission to go to the station to say goodbye to Miss Fothergill, that is, if the train was late enough so that school was out. Luckily the down-train was late, and all four girls went into the station waiting room together. Only Miss Fothergill and Mr. Guggums were there. She had put him on a pillow and thrown a shawl over his head, but Lucy saw the dog was shaking with a chill.

She went up to Miss Fothergill. "Is your old Mr. Guggums sick? I heard he was."

"The Langdon vet absolutely refused to come care for him, so I've paid to take him on my lap in the coach. He's a strong old chap, only I can't stay here with no medical attention for him." She wiped the dog's eyes with a corner of the shawl. "When the train comes, could you carry Mr. Guggums for me? I've got to see to my trunk and—Goodness, there's the whistle."

She stood up, handed Lucy the pillowful of dog, and loaded herself with two packages, a suitcase, and her handbag. Gwen picked up the other suitcase, and Gwin and Guinevere each picked up a small satchel. Out on the platform, the conductor took the bags from the girls and stacked them in the coach vestibule. Old Guggums was getting heavier and heavier in Lucy's arms, but when she tried to hand him and his pillow to the conductor, the man only shook his head and stepped over to talk to Tom Evans. Lucy climbed the two coach steps, waiting for Miss Fothergill, who was arguing about her trunk with the baggageman. By now the elephant of a dog was too much for Lucy, so she put him on his feet in the vestibule, but his old bow legs folded under him. Finally, she picked him up and boldly walked into the coach. At the first empty seat, she dumped her armload of dog and pillow and shawl and turned to run out again before the train carried her off to Langdon.

As she hurried across the vestibule, she looked directly into the smoker. Only one man sat in the whole smoking car, and he held a newspaper open in front of his face. But Lucy saw his hands. His right forefinger was crushed, exactly like hers, and like the finger on the hand of the detective's driver.

She jumped off, Miss Fothergill lumbered up the steps and called to the girls, "Thank you. Good-bye, and don't forget your poetry." The train began to clank, slowly move forward, and then after one whistle for the crossing, it was on its way.

Lucy watched it go, and having gotten into enough trouble in one spy hunt, she didn't speak to the others about the driver. But he was still a mystery man. She had never seen his face. "Yet he couldn't be a spy when he drives for a detective," she told herself. "Or could he be? And where's he going now?"

The next morning Mr. Grady came into the seventh-eighth grade room from his own high school room and brought Mary Hoffer with him. "This is your new teacher, and for the rest of the year in this schoolroom she'll be Miss Hoffer." He said the last two words very slowly. There was no nonsense about Mr. Grady, and he knew that Mary had grown up on a farm south of Wales. To hold the pupils' respect, she would have to be Miss Hoffer and not Mary.

From the moment he left and Miss Hoffer took charge, everything was different in Lucy's classes. As Gwen said later, "It's a turnabout for sure, isn't it?"

Miss Hoffer began with the class in reading. "The eighth grade needs so much work on *Hiawatha* to pass the state examinations in May that I'm combining the two grades for reading. Open your books to the lines, 'By the shores of Gitchie Gumee.' Who's ready to recite?"

Though several eighth grade girls put up their hands, Lenny Pearson was the only boy. Miss Hoffer nodded to him, he stood up, closed his book, and began a speech of his own. "Do you think that poet Longfellow ever saw an Indian? My pa hires Indians from the Reservation on our threshing crew, and they talk just as good as we do. If they ever heard me say this Gitchie Gumee stuff, they'd split themselves laughing. So what are we learning all this junk for?"

"Yah, that's what my folks want to know," Daisy Kohl said. "Last night I was studying out loud—and that line about the wild goose he calls Wawa got my pa so mad. He said to quit the babytalk and get to work."

Before Miss Hoffer could reply, Dale Schwinn was on his feet. "I say that poet never saw an Indian or the prairie either. He's got that line about the mountains in the land of the Dacotahs. That's not right, is it? We shouldn't have to learn wrong stuff in school."

They all began talking without first putting up their hands. "Who'd call a heron a Shuh-shuh-gah?" "Poetry's stupid." "We had poetry all the time and nothing else from Miss Fothergill." "It's all bunk!" shouted Cyril as the seventh grade began to take part in the revolt. "And we have to memorize two hundred lines—and why?"

"Why? Why? Why?" It was a chorus, echoing from the whole room.

"Keep still, all of you," Mary Hoffer ordered. "I'll tell you why you have to learn those two hundred lines. They are assigned for the state examination, and if you don't pass, you don't get your eighth grade diploma. That's why. When you've graduated from the eighth grade, you can ask me about this. Right now I have to get you through that state exam." She looked older and more severe than she ever had before. "Lenny, recite what you've memorized so far."

"Yes, ma'am," Lenny stood up and began to drone out "By the shores of Gitchie Gumee, By the shining Big-Sea-Water." And no one ever asked again about the mountains in the land of the Dacotahs or the Shuh-shuh-gah or the wild goose, Wawa.

Yet Mary Hoffer may have thought that poetry needed a firmer base than a Wawa. Since the state exams would include questions on North Dakota's history, she taught them about the fur traders, the early missionaries, and the Sioux and Crow Indians. Fifty miles east of Wales was Walhalla, one of the first settlements in Dakota. And even the boys liked the history of the Walhalla massacre. "Scalped those folks that didn't belong here! North Dakota Indians would have Gitchie-Gumeed Longfellow, wouldn't they?"

Unlike Miss Fothergill, Mary combined geography of Europe with the battle lines and allowed them to argue about the war, though the arguments often became shouting matches. "Wilson got elected to keep us out of war, and we'll stay out, too." "Germany's got the best army and all those U-boats. The Allies can't ever win." "My pa says it's Europe's mess, so why should we go in?"

Gwen, as a Canadian usually kept still, but at this, she spoke up. "My papa says America will soon go in."

Lucy agreed. "My father thinks the same. America will go to war. It's got to."

To quell the storm of no's and never's and not the USA!, Mary Hoffer took command. "I like your all having opinions and expressing them, but we must go on to spelling. For a review, Mitch, you spell ' believe ' and ' receive ' and give me the rule." Mitch rose at the back of the room to his six feet in height and slowly answered her.

This review of third and fourth grade work always sent Lucy off into daydreams. Even with Mary Hoffer as her teacher, Lucy was bored much of the time. She tried to hide her boredom by propping books in front of her, by occasionally catching Mary's eye and smiling brightly, but she knew she wasn't fooling Mary.

So she rather expected Mary to take her to task someday. But when Mary did speak to her after school one day early the next week, all she said was to ask her father if she could spend some of her time helping in another room. "I know he doesn't want you to teach two-times-two in the primary room again, but Mrs. O'Neil says she can use any tutoring she can get."

When Lucy explained that night to Father, he agreed, but he suggested that she listen more to the eighth grade work.

"They're just going over and over the stuff they have to know for the state exams, and I've listened until I could pass those exams in my sleep."

"Harry, what are we going to do with that child?" Lucy winced at Mother's calling her a child, but before she could object, Amory butted in.

"Make her skip a grade. You had me skip three, so I'd have to slave in school."

"When did you ever slave, Amory?" Mother laughed.

"And you know why you had to skip," Father said. "Remember in the first grade when the Dawson girls sat in front of you and you tied their long braids together—nearly scalped themselves before they discovered what you'd done."

"Oh, dear, yes," said Mother. "That teacher said you'd go or she would. And that was just the beginning of your school career. But about Lucy—we don't want her to skip any more. One grade was enough. Let her help in Mrs. O'Neil's room."

When Lucy did go down to the fourth-fifth-sixth

grade room, Mrs. O'Neil asked her to go to the empty seats at the back of the room and listen to Hilda Dickerman recite "The Children's Hour." "They're all learning something by Longfellow for the end-of-term program," Mrs. O'Neill explained, and Lucy tried to look pleased about more Longfellow. Over and over again, Hilda whispered the lines, always sticking on the list of the children's names—"Grave Alice, and laughing Allegra, And Edith with golden hair."

"Those lines aren't hard, Hilda. The poet's three girls, and one has blond hair, like yours."

"But what about the grave, Lucy? That's very sad," Hilda said softly.

"It's not a dead grave. It means she's the serious one." Then Lucy thought of the two little brothers that Hilda had buried. "Should I ask Mrs. O'Neil if you can learn a different poem?"

"No, I like it. A whole hour for the children, just for the children," Hilda repeated.

The next poem was about the village blacksmith, and it was like old times for Lucy to coach Willie Baumgarten on the lines "Under the spreading chestnut tree, The village smithy stands." She'd helped Willie the year before, and though he'd grown taller and taller, he hadn't advanced much in lessons. Yet a poem about a blacksmith he liked, only saying to Lucy, "Not much like the Wales blacksmith shop, is it? Bet Joe Klein's a better blacksmith. And did you ever see a chestnut tree?" Lucy had to admit she never had.

After that, Franz Schneider came to her. "I've been out sick, you know, so I'm way behind in measurement problems in the book."

"Let's start with this problem on the size of a barn," Lucy began. "You multiply the two sides and the height and—well, it's 75 rods by 50 by 75," she said.

Franz worked away at it, while Lucy looked out the window on the dirty snow in the schoolyard and wondered what a chestnut tree did look like. When she grew up, she'd travel and see—

"I got the answer, Lucy. But it seems awful big." Franz put his finger on the page. "Holy smoke! This barn would cover a whole farmyard! Lucy, did you see those are yards and not rods? Some barn!"

Lucy looked again and began to giggle, and Franz's shoulders began to shake, and then he let out a whoop of a laugh. It was the most noise Lucy had ever heard him make.

Mrs. O'Neil came down the aisle, and Lucy explained her mistake. "Franz knows more about the size of barns than I do."

"But the next problem is wallpapering a living room," Franz said. "I've got a lot to learn about wallpaper." And though Lucy considered wallpapering the stupidest of problems, she knew he had to master it to pass his grade. So together they calculated square foot after square foot of wallpaper, roll after roll, always allowing for the patterns to match.

"When I grow up, I'll not have an inch of wallpaper in my house," Lucy told him. "Not a single inch!"

"And when I have my own farm, I won't have a barn so big that I could lose a horse in it," Franz teased. Then as though he might have hurt her feelings, he said, "Thank you. You helped."

No one had made a point of thanking her before for tutoring, so she was tongue-tied a moment, as silent as Franz usually was. "Okay. I'll be back tomorrow," she replied and went upstairs to be dismissed with her own grade.

The War
Comes Closer

LUCY HAD BEEN so busy on the spy hunt and the changes at school that she'd almost forgotten about Lily Morgan, who had nearly died on New Year's Eve. Then one afternoon in mid-January she came home to find Mrs. Sanderson sitting in the living room with Mother.

Since Mrs. Sanderson knew everything that happened for thirty miles around, Lucy loved to sit quietly and listen while the two women talked. "Come pour us another cup of tea and have one yourself, Lucy," Mother invited. "We're celebrating because Lily Morgan is so much better that Mrs. Sanderson has her at her house. I want you to help her take home our two extra down pillows and that pale pink quilt we never use."

Both women were rocking in the two big chairs, close to the stove. Lucy drew up her own low rocker, first placing her cup and saucer on a low stool beside her.

"I really shouldn't stay any longer," Mrs. Sanderson said, as she put three teaspoons of sugar in her tea and stirred vigorously. "But I've been out at that Morgan farm so long without a soul to talk to that I'm wound up. Lily was too feeble to talk much, of course, and anyway she's so English that I couldn't always understand her. Once when I gave her a dish of porridge she said afterwards, 'I hate it,' and then I find it was just her extra *h*; but when she talked about living in the country instead of the city, she said, 'I ate it!' Well, you can't have much conversation that way, now can you?"

"Whatever will become of her?" Mother asked seriously. "Can Danny Morgan ever make a good husband? Or might she reform him? Harry has always said that that boy is better than his brother Mike· or his father, and Danny must have liked her to marry her."

"One thing's sure right now—though of course it may not last. He's really stuck on her, nearly went crazy when we thought she might die." Mrs. Sanderson lowered her voice. "I wouldn't want you to spread this because I'm not supposed to tell what happens at the bedside of my patients, but this isn't bad. It's good. When she was at her sickest and Dr. Carmer held out no hope, that Danny knelt beside her bed, and do you know what he said?"

Mother said nothing and Lucy's eyes were riveted on Mrs. Sanderson. "He said, 'God don't let her die. Take me instead.' "

"Danny Morgan said that?"

"Yes, he did, Mrs. Johnston. And the doctor said to

me that he didn't know any Morgan used the name of God except to swear. This last week, you should have seen him tend her as gently as a woman."

"Well, I never!" Mother exclaimed. And Lucy found herself swiftly rearranging her opinion of Danny Morgan, though Mrs. Sanderson had nothing good to say of old man Morgan or the other son, Mike.

"Pair of crooks, those two are. Glad they cleared out when I came to stay. Probably they were in town here, running that filthy saloon."

"I don't know that Lucy's heard it, but Harry tells me that Mike disappeared on New Year's Night. Afraid he'd be caught for some shady business, even shadier than the blind pig. Did you hear anything about it?"

"No, and out there would be the last place I'd hear, I suppose." Mrs. Sanderson rose, put on her things, warned Mother to care for herself, and after Lucy had dressed again to go out, the two of them set off with pillows and quilt, looking like a bedding display. At her front door, Mrs. Sanderson explained, "Danny's here, watching over Lily while I went to see your Mother. Come on in and help me unload." As she put her hand on the knob, the door was opened for them by Danny, about to leave.

"Glad you came just now. I got a phone call and have to meet somebody," he said. He looked different to Lucy, more like his cousin Luke, who was for Lucy "the good Morgan," but whether he had changed because she'd heard something good about him or whether it was only his calling back to Lily, "I'll be with you again soon, sweet," Lucy wasn't sure.

The downstairs bedroom was next to the door, and Mrs. Sanderson led the way in there. Sitting up in the brass bedstead with blankets wrapped around her was

Lily Morgan, and instantly Lucy recognized her. She was a young Canadian war widow whom Lucy and Mother had talked to during the summer. Then she was sick with fear, fear of the lonely woods around the remote farm on the Pembina River, where her husband's parents lived. Now she was sick but gradually getting well, and her fears were gone. She was as pale as before and even thinner, yet she looked happy, totally and completely happy.

Mrs. Sanderson introduced Lucy and propped Lily higher with the extra pillows, while Lily babbled about their plans. "We've been talking about which city we'll go to. Now it's Halifax, we think. Lots of war jobs, and I can work too. And isn't it lucky he's a Canadian so it can be Halifax?" And both times Lily called it *Alifax*.

"Goodness, that medicine from the drugstore," Mrs. Sanderson broke in. "I meant to have Danny get it, but —Lucy, your mother can spare you a few minutes longer. Could you run quickly and get it? I should have given it to you an hour ago, Lily."

So Lucy set off at a run, and since it seemed to be an emergency, she chanced the short cut past the blind pig. It was already dusk and a lamp was burning inside the place, but the light showed only a moment. Then a hand of someone inside pulled down the shade to the windowsill. What was astonishing to Lucy was that she clearly saw that the hand had a crushed forefinger.

Later she told Mother all about Lily, and Mother agreed it must be the young woman from London, but Lucy told no one about the mystery man. After all, she shouldn't have been on that path, and anyway, what could she say about a man whose face she'd never seen.

Father had promised the Boy Scouts a night meeting

in the igloo that Friday, but when all the candles and the food and the ropes for practising knots were piled in the shed, the weather suddenly changed to a January thaw, and the igloo shrank all day Thursday. By Friday night it was a melted heap of porous snow and old boards. The boys complained. Father was apologetic. And the Owens politely said nothing but looked a great many I-told-you-so's when they saw the ruin. For Mother the thaw was a boon, not only because everyone had caught a sore throat or a cold in the igloo and now the igloo was no more, but because she could walk outdoors again, even going to Main Street on Friday for the mail.

"Look what I've got for you," Mother called, as Lucy came out of the school and caught up to her. Mother drew from her fur muff a shiny colored postcard with rough edges, quite unlike any card bought in Wales or anywhere in the United States. The picture was of a village with a bumpy stone street. "Cobblestones," Lucy said aloud, "the kind you read about." Over the shops hung signs in a foreign language, though one word was familiar: "Hotel" in fancy letters on a swinging carved board. Turning the card over, she saw it was addressed to her, and when she checked the signature, she exclaimed, "Mother, it's from Luke Morgan and it says 'Have a Merry Christmas!' Awfully long getting here, wasn't it?"

"Don't forget it had to cross the Atlantic in wartime," Mother said.

"He's in France now," Lucy went on. "Oh dear, he's really in the war."

"Soldiers do go to war, Lucy," Mother said consolingly, "and many of them come home, good as ever."

"Did you read it all, even the P.S., Mother? He says

'P.S. Your brother's cave prepared me for the trenches. So here's a thank-you. I'll come to see you when the war's over.' "

"I wish I'd met him," Mother said. "Your father will be glad he's still fine."

"Fine?" Lucy repeated, but she was thinking of what she'd read of the winter trenches in France, of the mud and the cold and the filth and the rats and the steady bombardment and the barbed wire entanglements the soldiers had to go through when they went over the top. "Mr. Owen says the Canadians have been in the worst battles this winter. He reads those casualty lists, and he says a lot won't come home."

A week later at supper, Father spoke of Mr. Owen's Canadian newspaper with its sad long casualty list. "Did it include Manitoba?" Lucy asked. "Luke's name wasn't on it, was it?" Then she added, "But he must be all right. I got that card from him just last week."

"You'll have to know it sooner or later. He's not on that list, but Danny Morgan came in today to see about selling his share of the farm and—"

"And what did he tell you?" Lucy wanted to know, and she didn't want to know.

"Luke never fought in the war at all. He caught pneumonia in France, and last month, crossing the Channel to England, his hospital ship was sunk by a U-boat. Every man was lost."

"He was dead when I got my card from him? He's gone? Luke Morgan?" Lucy understood, yet the puzzling part was how he died. "He drowned? And pneumonia? Why he could have stayed at home and died of that. Poor Luke." She'd seen him only the one afternoon when she'd helped him hide in Amory's cave until dark, but he'd lived in her imagination ever since.

And now that was the only place he would continue to live.

On the morning of the second of February everybody was in his seat in Lucy's room before the last bell rang. Beginning as usual, Mary Hoffer said, "Both grades, take out your *Hiawatha* books."

Lenny Pearson waved his hand, stood up, and spoke all in the same instant. "Instead of that Shuh-shuh-gah stuff, let's talk about the news. What's—

"Yah, what's the USA going to do?" Cyril interrupted. "Germany says we got to paint our ships like sticks of candy—big red and white stripes and—"

Julie Meizner jumped up and shouted, "And we got to fly a red and white checkerboard flag like our kitchen tablecloth. Won't we have our own flag any more?"

"Stop shouting and let me ask some questions," Mary commanded. "What else did Germany demand?" No one answered. "It's more important than the candy stripes. Listen to me. Germany says we can send only one ship across the ocean each week, and it can sail only where she'll let it go." Mary paused. "Gwendolyn, you must know what's so important about that."

"The people in France and England are hungry." Gwen stood quietly beside her desk, and she spoke quietly too. "The German U-boats are sinking every ship on the seas, and soon no food will get to the Allies. Then the people will starve, and Germany will win." Gwen sat down. Mary quickly changed the subject.

"Now for *Hiawatha*," Mary said, but Mr. Grady knocked and came in with two cages of white mice that his science class was feeding to prove facts about food.

"I thought you'd all like to see how puny this batch of mice is—not eating the right things. And then look at this cageful, sturdy and frisky and sleek. Now they're getting a good diet." He walked up and down the aisles, telling everyone what was a good diet for people too. The boys kept asking questions, trying to postpone *Hiawatha*. But most of the girls were glad to see Mr. Grady carry his cages back to his own room.

"I think we'll get to *Hiawatha*," Mary began again. Mamie Schmidt waved her hand so hard that Mary had to notice her.

"We can't stop those candy stripes, but pretty soon it's Valentine's Day. That's important too. Will we have a box?"

"Yes, we'll celebrate, no matter what the Kaiser or the President does." Mary laughed so that the crinkles came around her eyes, and everyone laughed with her. "But this year, Mrs. O'Neil's room has invited us downstairs, and she asks that all the valentines be homemade. And now—*Hiawatha!*" She grinned, but she meant business.

For days after that Lucy and the girls made valentines. Mother donated packages of lace paper doilies, and Father brought from the barn attic some rolls of fancy old wallpaper. The Boy Scouts teased them about kindergarten work until the girls plotted a revenge. Lucy copied instructions for tying Scout knots, and secretly the girls practised the reef knot, the double halfhitch, the bowline—every knot that the boys considered impossible for girls.

Outdoors it was so bitterly cold that not even the boys put on skates and looked for ice on a ditch. The girls were always in school or in the house, but they never grew bored with one another. Now and then, Lucy said to herself, "What can I do when they're gone away? My prophecy had better come true!"

A Quiet
Boy

BECAUSE OF the homemade valentines, the celebration in Mrs. O'Neil's room was more fun than usual. She had made heart-shaped cookies by the hundreds, all frosted in red, and the valentines were cutouts and paste-ups and drawings. Even the boys had made a few, but mostly for each other and all funny ones. For Lucy the surprise was a thick, folded brown paper valentine that she had to open and open again and again until it was spread across two desks and an aisle. When she saw what it was, everyone around her laughed and she looked over at Franz and called, "Our barn gets bigger all the time, doesn't it?" She wished she had made him one and used yards of wallpaper in it. It hadn't occurred to her.

What happened in the next few days happened so

swiftly that Lucy wasn't aware it was happening until it was all over. On Friday, when she went down to Mrs. O'Neil's room, she helped Hilda with her reading and Willie with his fractions and Tina Meizner with the state capitals. But Franz wasn't in school. At recess she asked Peter about him. "How come Franz's not in school. Is he sick again?"

"Him and Rose are both sick. He's got that pain like last month, so he stayed home."

Saturday night, when the Boy Scouts were meeting in the dining room, mostly for Ping Pong and popcorn, Mrs. Sanderson phoned to ask if Stan could stay overnight with Amory. Father answered, and in the silence as the *bip-bop* of the Ping Pong balls stopped, Lucy heard the worry in Father's voice. "Who's sick out at Schneiders'?" Then Lucy heard the word, "Franz."

"He's young," Father said. "He'll make it all right, but now's when we need a hospital. Call us when you get back tomorrow morning." Later Father answered their questions briefly and seriously. "His appendix, and Dr. Carmer's operating out at the farm."

The next morning Mrs. Sanderson didn't phone, but Mrs. Carmer did. Father said nothing until he was beside Mother, in the other room. "The doctor phoned home. No chance of getting the boy over a hundred miles to the hospital, and the appendix was ruptured." Father spoke very low, but Lucy heard him, and as soon as Father had taken the boys out to ski on barrel-stave skis, Lucy asked Mother more about Franz. "Isn't a ruptured appendix awfully serious? Doesn't that mean the poison goes all through the person and kills him?" They were standing by the range in the cozy kitchen, doing dishes together, and the words sounded like something in a book, not like Wales.

"Let's leave the rest of the dishes to dry," Mother said, "and we'll go sit by the stove." Once in her rocking chair, she did answer Lucy's question. "He's very sick. There's no use in fooling you. The doctor may not be able to save him."

"Could he live if they got him to a hospital? I know it's a hundred and fifty miles to the big hospital in Grand Forks, but it's only half that far to the little one in Devil's Lake. Couldn't they make a bed in a box sleigh and wrap him up warm?"

"Look out the window at the road, at the ruts and the ice and the snow. And farther south there might be mud with the snow. He'd never survive the trip."

"Will he die because we have no hospital? Because we've got only Dr. Carmer?"

"Don't talk that way about Dr. Carmer. He's such a good doctor that if it weren't for his one bad habit he wouldn't be in a village. He'll do the best any doctor can do." Mother picked up her sewing. "Look, Lucy, I've started a pink baby blanket for you to work on, and I'll finish the blue one."

It was dusk and the boys and Father were home, when a team and sleigh stopped. Before Mrs. Sanderson was at the door, Father had swung it open and called, "You bring good news, I hope."

Mrs. Sanderson stepped inside and closed the door behind her. Lucy and Amory and Stan rushed to her, and Mother came slowly to the living room doorway.

Pushing down the scarf that covered the lower part of her face, Mrs. Sanderson put her other hand on Stan's shoulder. Her voice quivered. "Bad news. Franz died about an hour ago. It was hopeless from the first." She reached into the deep pocket of her dark blue coat, took out her handkerchief and began to cry. Always

Lucy had seen her as the practical nurse, the one who always knew what to do and always cheered everyone else.

Stan put his arm around her waist. "Let's go home, Ma," he said, and suddenly he seemed far older than Amory. "We kept the stoves going so it's warm, and I'll make you some tea."

Mother took off her glasses to wipe the tears that were rolling down her cheeks, and Father was strangely white. His voice that was sometimes so gruff and loud was soft and gentle. "We'd be glad to have you and Stan stay here."

"No, you were good to keep him today, but now it's time for him and me to go home, together." Stan immediately put on his red mackinaw and plaid cap, she pulled up her scarf again, and with her arm around him they went out into the early dark of the February night.

Lucy had heard everything, but nothing seemed true until Amory spoke. "A kid just as old as Lucy, and he's dead."

Even then she said to herself, "Franz Schneider—he couldn't be dead."

Around the living room stove, the four of them stood so close that they were almost scorched, seeking heat to warm themselves. Lucy was the first to ask a question. "Do you think a hospital in Wales or even twenty miles away in Langdon—do you think then he wouldn't be dead?"

Father answered very soberly. "Lucy, you always want an answer for everything, and sometimes there is no answer. But this time—yes, in a good operating room in a good hospital even in Langdon, twenty miles away, Franz might have lived. But don't say that to

Peter or to anyone. It's no comfort now."

Mother wiped her eyes once more, put her glasses back on, and said, "Harry, you and the children get yourselves some supper. I don't think I want—"

"You must, Caroline. For the baby."

"Of course. A bowl of crackers and milk, please, Lucy."

In the morning, Lucy was almost late to school because Mother asked her to do so many things. When she finally had the breakfast dishes done, the covers jerked across the beds and the extra coal shoveled on each fire, Lucy pulled on her galoshes, dragged her scarf from the sleeve of her coat, jammed on her knit cap, shoved her arms into her coat sleeves, called good-bye to Mother, and tore out the back door, with only four minutes to run along the rim of the snowbanks to school. As the last bell finished its last *ding-dong*, Lucy puffed up the stairs at full speed, yanking off her coat and cap as she went.

She hung them on the nearest empty peg in the hall and opened the door of her room. Everyone was sitting silent, head bowed and hands clasped. Mary Hoffer put her finger to her lips. Lucy slipped into her front seat and copied what everyone else was doing. Then as she clasped her hands on the desk in front of her, she understood what was going on. The class was saying a prayer for Franz.

After a minute or two, Mary stood up and said, "Though Franz was not a pupil in this room, we all knew him, and we all know his brother Peter and his sister Rose, and we all know his parents. In a few days there will be a funeral mass, and I hope most of the school can go. Franz was good and kind and the sort of boy who makes friends in a quiet way. Now we'll begin classes."

And still Lucy had not cried, though some of the girls around her were crying, and even the boys were sober and attentive to Mary's orders. At eleven o'clock, Mary nodded to Lucy that it was time to go down to Mrs. O'Neil's room. So when the tan geography books were shoved into the desks and the blue spelling books were opened, Lucy went out the door and down the worn wooden stairs to Mrs. O'Neil's room.

There it happened. Lucy stepped inside. Mrs. O'Neil was putting penmanship models on the board for the fourth grade, the sixth grade was at the side blackboard doing percentage problems, and only the fifth grade was sitting in their seats. And right at the end of the farthest row was the empty seat where Franz should have been. Lucy's lips began to quiver; she caught her breath in a grating sob, and she began to cry out loud. She got no farther than just inside the door, and there she stood, crying in front of a whole room. They stared at her, and some of the girls began to cry with her. She needed a handkerchief and didn't have one. She couldn't back out, and she couldn't go in.

Mrs. O'Neil turned when she heard the sobs, came directly to Lucy's side, put her arm around her and led her to the hall. There she gave Lucy her handkerchief, waited until the crying had lessened and then asked, "Maybe you'd like to go home? I'll explain to Miss Hoffer."

"Yes, yes. I don't want to be anywhere but home," Lucy said between her choking and sobbing.

"You need your mother. Go upstairs quietly and be sure to put on all your things—you mustn't freeze." She stooped, gave Lucy a kiss and watched her go up the stairs.

At home, Mother was playing the piano. "Lucy? Home so early?" she called, as she broke off her music with a finishing chord.

Fearful lest she begin to cry again, Lucy didn't answer. She took off her things, dipped a basin of warm water from the range-reservoir and washed her face, drying it on the long white roller towel on the door. Then she went in to Mother.

"I cried. I cried and I couldn't stop—right in front of Mrs. O'Neil's three grades, when I went to tutor. Mother, he'll never, never be there again. And I didn't make him a valentine." Her tears began flowing again.

"Better to cry some of it out. I was sitting here crying myself until I began to play. Listen—I'll sit here and play you some of the music that made me feel better." And while Lucy sat curled up in Father's big chair, Mother gave her a special concert.

For Franz's funeral the little Catholic church was packed with nearly everyone from the village and the countryside, including all the older school children. Lucy had been at Catholic mass before, since Mother sometimes played the organ when no Catholic musician could come. But this time the mass didn't seem so long and boring as it had before. To her the service now had a purpose. As Mother had said, "It's a farewell to Franz." And Father Van Mert was her old friend, though dressed in his church robes he looked more like a painting than like a person, and certainly not like a man who enjoyed his pet crow.

All the Schneiders and their relatives were in deep mourning. Peter, very tall in his new black suit, was a pallbearer and helped carry the coffin in and out. A lot of the women cried and even some of the school children, but not Lucy. The Franz she mourned was the quiet boy in Mrs. O'Neil's room, sitting in his seat at the back. That boy wasn't here.

From then on she asked not to go downstairs to tutor. But this created a new problem. How was Lucy to fill her school hours? Mary Hoffer had only one suggestion, which she didn't tell Lucy. Instead she wrote it and put it in a sealed envelope for Lucy to carry home on Friday afternoon.

"What do you suppose it says?" Gwin asked. "Can you see through the envelope?"

Lucy held it up to the sun, but nothing showed through, so Gwen said, "We'll come along with you, and maybe your mother will tell you what it's about."

"Not likely," Lucy answered. "Mary Hoffer said my folks should make the decision, and that always means my father."

"Here, girls—fresh molasses cookies," Mother welcomed them. "Quick, before those three Boy Scouts get here. They're going skating on the slough behind Mrs. Bortz's house." Lucy handed her the envelope from school and watched Mother read the letter. "Hmmmmm," Mother said. Then she looked at the page again. And again she said, "Hmmmmm."

Before she had time to read it a third time, Lucy asked, "What's it about?"

"I want to think about it, and so will your father." Mother put the note back in the envelope and tucked it into her apron pocket. Then Amory and Jerry and Stan literally blew in, and Mother scolded, "Shut that door! It's not spring yet. Have some cookies; and

Amory, I've put your skate key on this strong cord. Your skates won't clamp to your boots without it, so don't lose it."

"Can't we go?" asked Gwin.

"It's for boys," Jerry scoffed.

"After five minutes, girls always yowl about frozen toes or faces. Anyway they can't clamp skates on their sissy galoshes," Amory said between cookies. Then all yelling together the boys ran out through the shed. In a moment, Amory dashed in again, grabbed his skate key from the kitchen table, and raced out, slamming the kitchen door just as Mother called out, "Shut that door!"

To the girls Mother then said, "Did you want to go?"

"Not really," Lucy answered. "The boys are right about clamping on skates. I have to clamp them on my shoes, and then without galoshes my feet are frigid. I wish I could wear boots like the boys. You folks say that boys and girls should be able to do the same things, but how can I without boots?"

"Amory's got an outgrown pair. You can wear them to school next week, if you like."

"That's the advantage of an older brother," Gwen said. Sometimes the Owen girls envied Lucy because she had Amory, and sometimes Lucy wished they had him, just long enough to see what life with Amory was like. Yet she knew that after he had gone away to school, home would be very dull. Always when she thought of that, she said over and over to herself, "My prophecy, my secret prophecy—come true, come true."

Waiting

AT SUPPERTIME Amory came in at the same time Father did. Amory's whole cheek was marble white. "Frostbite," Father said the moment he looked at it. "Lucy, get a pan of snow. If the outdoors freezes him, then the outdoors should cure." Father rubbed the cheek with snow, Mother warned Amory to stay away from the hot stove because too fast a thawing is painful, and even Lucy forgot the note.

Later at the table Mother handed the note to Father. "Mary sent this home, sealed. It's for us to decide."

Father took it, and while he read, Amory's cheek was so thawed that he began to tease. "Bet Mary wants to get rid of you. Back to the sixth grade, Lucy."

Mother shook her head at him. "Be quiet while your father thinks."

Father began exactly as Mother had. "Hmmmmm," and then a second "Hmmmmm. Mary says you probably should skip to the eighth grade. I suppose she sealed it because if we decided against it, you'd better not know at all."

"Lucy, you'll never pass those state exams in May," Amory warned. "I thought they'd be easy, but they were bad, with tricky questions about wars and dates in history that I knew but you'd fall on your face." It was true that Amory's specialty was history, but Lucy wasn't about to agree with him.

"Amory, this is Lucy's decision—and ours, not yours," Mother hushed him. "Mary suggests that your father go to school for an hour or so and listen to the two grades before any decision is made."

Lucy looked fiercely at Father. "If you come to my room that way, everybody'll know what you came for. I'd hate that! If you do it, I won't open my mouth, I won't read out loud, I won't recite poems, I won't do arithmetic on the blackboard, I won't go to the map for geography, I won't—"

"Wait!" Father stopped her. "I don't intend to waste my time in your schoolroom. It's your decision. Do you want to stay in the seventh grade or skip to the eighth?"

"I've made up my mind. I want to skip, right away."

"Don't say I didn't warn you about those state exams," Amory preached. "When you fail, you'll be sad, very sad."

"The only sad thing, Lucy, is that you'll have only two more years at home. And with the new baby, I'd love to have you here," Mother said.

"Oh, she'll be big when I leave in 1919," Lucy began.

"Yes," Amory interrupted. "He'll be a whopper by

then. How about betting on whether it'll be a girl or a boy?"

"No betting on this baby," Father said decisively. "If he-she is born healthy and strong, we all win."

But later on when Mother had gone to bed early and Father was working at his desk in the dining room, Amory whispered, "Come on, I'll bet you a dollar it's a boy."

"I never have dollars," Lucy replied.

"This is the way to get one. You might win," Amory said, "especially since that northern lights spell guarantees you're lucky." So Lucy agreed, but she had a feeling that no spell would win a bet from Amory.

Before school on Monday morning, Lucy had to wait while Mother wrote a reply to Mary, and after that Mother reminded her that she'd wanted to wear Amory's outgrown boots to school. When Lucy had put them on and laced them up, she saw how scuffed and worn they were, with one toe split through the outer layer and both boots coated with last year's mud.

But she had no time to change again and hurried to meet the Owens at their house. There Edward was starting off to school in his new boots, very grand in comparison to her hand-me-downs. He took one look at her feet and began to yell, "Look! Lootsie's got bootsies!" and he yelled all the rest of the block to school and into the schoolyard. "Lootsie's got boot-sies! Lootsie's got bootsies!"

Lucy could have killed him on the spot. Gwen tried to hush him, Gwin laughed and thought it very funny, and Guinevere corrected him, "Edward, her name's Lucy, not Lootsie. That's baby talk."

At noon Lucy changed to her own shoes and threw the boots into the closet corner. Boots were one more advantage that boys had, she decided, and no girl could do everything a boy could do, no matter what Father said.

Afterwards it was those clumping boots that Lucy remembered about that day, and not her promotion into the eighth grade. Mary read the note from Mother, nodded to Lucy, pointed to an empty seat at the front of the eighth-grade rows, and asked her, "Can you see the blackboard as well there?" Lucy was so short that she never escaped a front seat no matter what grade she was in. Once Lucy had moved her books and papers to that desk, with no announcement made, she simply began reciting in the eighth grade classes in every subject.

Perhaps skipping a grade would have been more exciting if it hadn't been March, the month for the birth of the baby. Every morning Lucy woke wondering whether this would be the birthday of her new sister, but by evening there was no new baby. Mother grew bigger and bigger. Lucy ran more errands, made more beds and swept more floors than ever before, but still no baby.

Amory said he'd done so many dishes that he thought he'd take a job in a restaurant and get paid, only Wales had no restaurant. And every night Father left about eight o'clock, first telling them to phone him at his office if Mother needed him.

Lucy thought Father must be doing extra work at the bank, but one evening at supper the phone rang, Lucy answered, and it was Dr. Carmer. He spoke abruptly and in a great rush. "Tell your father I can't play cards tonight. Mrs. Foster, east of town, is having a baby, so I'll be out there all night." And he hung up.

Back at the table, Lucy reported the message and then looked hard at Father. "Have you been playing cards every night with the doctor when we thought you were working?"

"Is it poker and how much do you bet and who wins?" Amory asked.

Mother said only, "Harry, you might as well explain."

"Yes, I do play cards with the doctor every night now, and no, we don't bet money."

"Isn't it boring? And does the doctor drink?" Amory kept on.

"This baby is overdue. There's no other way we can be sure Dr. Carmer will be sober when the baby does come. Your poor father is doing it for me. He's a real martyr!" Mother smiled across the table at him.

"Other people's babies don't dawdle this long, do they?" Lucy asked.

"I've done enough dishes to reach from here to the moon and—"

Before Amory could enumerate all his hard work, Mother interrupted. "You two stop complaining. I'm rather tired of waiting too. But some day you'll come home from school and Mrs. Sanderson will hand you a baby wrapped in a new blanket, for you to hold a moment or two, at least."

But that wasn't exactly how it happened. Two nights later, Father was down at the office playing cards with Dr. Carmer. Lucy and Mother had gone to bed. "Lucy, Lucy, have Amory phone your father to bring the doctor and Mrs. Sanderson, too. Hurry."

Lucy ran down the stairs so fast that she nearly tripped, and as she ran, she called, "Amory, get Father and the doctor and Mrs. Sanderson—get everybody, quick!"

By the time she was at the bottom of the stairs, he

was at the wall telephone, cranking the two rings for the bank on their private line. "The baby's coming!" he yelled into the black mouthpiece. "Mother wants everybody—the baby's coming!"

By now Lucy was also in the dining room, and she heard Father's shout, "We'll be there!" Then Lucy ran back upstairs. "Everybody's on the way," Lucy said through Mother's closed door. "Do you need me?"

"No, my dear," Mother answered shakily. "You just go down to the kitchen range and have Amory help you push forward that big kettle of water onto the hottest part of the stove."

While Lucy and Amory were in the kitchen, Father rushed in, and without taking off his cap or his coat, he bounded up the stairs to the bedroom. Lucy could hear the low rumble of his voice, but no more. Then Dr. Carmer hurried in. He was usually very polite, but this time without even so much as a hello, he ran up to the bedroom almost as fast as Father had.

Amory and Lucy stood by the range, saying nothing and feeling as though a couple of cyclones had whirled by them.

Next there was a knock on the outer shed door. Amory scooted out to open it. "Come on in, Mrs. Sanderson. Everybody's here but the baby, and maybe he's here now too." Mrs. Sanderson bustled into the kitchen, checked the kettle of water, asked Lucy for newspapers, and then laying aside her coat and hat, she also disappeared up the stairs.

"Newspapers!" Amory said. "Is she going to read the news to Mother or is that boy going to be wrapped in yesterday's *Grand Forks Herald?*"

Lucy felt very superior as she explained. "Mother's told me quite a bit about what goes on when a baby's born. The papers are to protect the mattress. A birth's very watery, you know."

"Oh, yeah, I forgot. You could say that babies swim before they do anything else, couldn't you?"

Soon Father was downstairs again, hung up his coat, warmed his hands at the range, and looked at Amory and Lucy. "You'll get more sleep at some other house tonight. Stan's alone, so Mrs. Sanderson suggests you go there. Bundle yourselves up warmly and run along."

"I thought it was only little kids that had to leave when—"

Father's face turned to a thundercloud, and Amory never finished his argument. "You two will do what I say," Father ordered. Then he relented enough to add. "This house is too small for a mother in childbirth, a doctor, a nurse and the father, too. I know you and Lucy aren't little kids, but there simply isn't room for everyone here. Now good night to both of you."

When Amory and Lucy knocked at the Sandersons' door, Stan let them in. "So the new baby threw you out? I'll take you in. You crawl in beside me tonight, Amory. And Lucy, you can sleep downstairs in Ma's bed for her patients."

Before she fell asleep, huddled in the chilly bed, Lucy thought of the last time she'd been in that room. Lily and Danny Morgan had left now for eastern Canada. "For 'Alifax," Lucy mumbled to herself. She'd overheard Father say to Mother, "If Danny ever does amount to anything, it will be because that girl made him go away." So, thought Lucy, for some people going away is good. Then she put her mind on what was happening at home.

Early in the morning Amory woke her. "Get up, Lucy. I'm going home to see what's happened." Lucy threw back the covers, dressed without washing her face or combing her hair, threw on her coat and followed Amory out the door and along the board sidewalk toward home.

It was barely light, a windy gray March morning. At the back gate they met Mrs. Sanderson, on her way home. "I'm going home to rest a little. I've left some hot cereal on the stove for your breakfast and—"

Lucy interrupted. "The baby! What about the baby?"

"Not born yet. In fact, for the last few hours, he's stopped trying to be born. The doctor's still there, of course." Lucy wanted to ask more about Mother, but Mrs. Sanderson walked briskly away.

When they came in, Father and Dr. Carmer were having coffee in the dining room. Father spoke almost in a whisper. "Get your dishes of oatmeal and eat here with us."

Later the doctor whispered, "Good morning, and I'm sorry there's no baby here for you to see." Lucy and Amory nodded silently, and Father went upstairs on tiptoe.

Soon he was down again. "Your mother would like to see you both before you go to school, but don't stay more than a minute or two. She's exhausted."

Together they went up. Amory knocked softly, and Mother answered, "I'm all right, children. Come in." Stepping into the room, Lucy first felt the warmth of the little round portable oil stove and smelled the stinging odor of disinfectant. Then she saw Mother, lying back on a fresh pillowcase, with her hair in two long, neat braids and the pink plaid blanket pulled up close around her shoulders. Lucy saw that she wore her best flannel nightie with the white embroidery around the

neck, but Mother's face was drawn and her eyes looked weak without her glasses.

"Give me a kiss, each of you. It's a very slowpoke baby, isn't it?" she said, smiling faintly. "You both look as though you needed to comb your hair and wash. Do that, and go off to school. I'll be right here when you get back, and maybe somebody else will be, too."

When Lucy stopped at the parsonage on the way to school, Mrs. Owen called from the kitchen the moment the door opened. "Is it a boy or a girl?"

"Neither! Slowest baby I ever heard of."

"It'll come, sooner or later. They always do," Mrs. Owen tried to cheer her. "How's your mother?"

"Sort of resting while she waits. The doctor's still there, and my father isn't going to the bank at all this morning." Suddenly Lucy realized that this was a sign of how worried Father must be. "Mrs. Owen, do you think the baby's being so slow could mean my mother might die?"

"No, Lucy, actually this baby isn't slower than a lot of them, and even when babies are born in a hospital, fathers stay near. Don't worry. Everything will be all right." Not until later did Lucy remember that she and Mrs. Owen had discussed the baby and Mother. The girls hadn't said a word. They didn't know what to say —not even Gwen.

"Perhaps it's begun to happen to me, the growing up that happens to women but never to men," Lucy said to herself as she thought of her talk with Mrs. Owen. "Maybe I'm changing more than any of them."

The
New Baby

AT NOON Lucy beat Amory into the house. Mrs. Sanderson was ladling corn chowder into the soup plates. She looked up, smiled, but didn't say a word. So Lucy didn't bother to ask about a baby. "How's Mother?" was her only question.

"Worn out," Mrs. Sanderson replied. "It's a hard birth. You two children are old enough to be told that much."

"But she'll be all right, won't she?" Lucy paused. "She's not going to—"

"Yes, she'll be all right." Then Mrs. Sanderson went on more seriously. "You must know that having a baby when a woman's along in her forties—like your mother —isn't easy."

Amory took his chowder to the dining room to eat

with Father and Dr. Carmer. Lucy lingered near Mrs. Sanderson. "Did Mother know it would be so hard for her?"

"Of course she did, but she probably talked to you only about the fun of a new baby."

"I'm scared, Mrs. Sanderson, awfully scared."

"There's your chowder. Go on in and eat, Lucy. Either you're a terrible worrier or too thin-skinned to live in this world." Then she changed from scolding to smiling. "All you have to do is wait a little longer."

After dinner Father sent Amory to Main Street for groceries. Lucy began to wash the dishes, and Mrs. Sanderson went upstairs. When she came down, she said, "Your mother wants to see you before you go back to school."

Lucy went up and softly rapped on Mother's door. "Yes? Come, Lucy." Mother's voice was very faint. Lucy went in. The bedroom was not neat and orderly as it had been that morning. There were pitchers and bottles and two slop jars, and tossed over Mother was an old threadbare gray blanket. Instead of the pink nightie, she had on a wrinkled rough white gown, tied at the neck with a tape. Her hair was damp around her forehead, and her face was perspiring and slack. She tried a smile, but it was such a weary one that it only frightened Lucy.

"Mrs. Sanderson says you're worried, my dear. Look, I'm right here, and I'll soon be fine." Then her mouth twisted and she moaned in pain. "Ohhh, ohhh, ohhh! Get the doctor."

Both the doctor and Mrs. Sanderson went up as fast as Lucy had come down. Father held out Lucy's coat for her to go to school, and all he said was, "Tell

Amory to leave the groceries in the shed and go directly to school."

By four o'clock, Lucy felt as though the afternoon session had lasted a week. When dismissal came, Lucy pushed rudely out of the room, elbowing aside not only Cyril and Harvey and all the boys, but the girls as well, including Gwen. She snatched her coat, put it under her arm, and was the first one out of the school door. Along the block past the parsonage and the Methodist church, across the road, past Kinsers' and Flints' and Mrs. Schnitzler's and through her back gate she ran. Along the back walk, through the back shed and into the kitchen she flew.

She closed the door behind her quietly and leaned against it to catch her breath. Mrs. Sanderson was bending over the kitchen table with something blanketed in her hands. She looked up at Lucy with a wide smile. "Your mother's all right, and he's here!"

"*He's* here? A boy? Instead of a baby sister I've got another brother?"

"Of course a *he's* a boy. Never heard of one that wasn't." Mrs. Sanderson laughed at Lucy's shocked expression. "Aren't you glad about your mother?"

"Yes, I'm glad about Mother, but she went through all that for another boy?"

"Oh, come, Lucy! Complain to me if you like, but don't you say a word to your mother about your disappointment. Here, hold him a moment and you'll feel better about him."

Lucy put out her arms and took the tiny roll of blankets. She looked down and saw a purple-red, tiny squeezed-up face. Now and then Mother had taken her to see new babies, but this was the homeliest baby she'd ever laid eyes on. "Maybe it's lucky he isn't a girl," she murmured as she returned him to Mrs. Sanderson.

"Give him time, and he's got to grow. Weighs only about five pounds now." Mrs. Sanderson readjusted the blankets and put him in his basket on two chairs near the range.

"Five pounds is puny, isn't it?" Lucy asked. The girls at school were always bragging about new babies that weighed nine or even ten pounds.

"Your mother says you and Amory weren't very hefty babies."

Amory came in and in a foghorn whisper asked, "Is that kid here yet?" Then he glanced toward the basket, saw the roll of blankets and in a second he was leaning over to stare. "Gosh! Must be a girl to be so homely." He shook his head glumly.

Lucy didn't like the insult, but neither did she want to tell him he'd won his bet. Mrs. Sanderson told him. "Not a girl at all. It's your new brother."

"I won my bet!" Amory crowed, and Mrs. Sanderson immediately hushed him, and also warned him not to tell Mother if he was disappointed.

"But I'm not," Amory assured her. "I bet Lucy a dollar he'd be a boy."

"He is a boy, but he weighs only five pounds and that means I'd pay you twenty cents a pound—seems a lot for . . ."

Father and Dr. Carmer came down the stairs, both smiling as though they'd produced the baby. "Well, how do you like him," asked Dr. Carmer, as Father helped him on with his coat.

"I wanted a girl, dreadfully," Lucy began, "but anyway we're done waiting. That's something."

The doctor laughed and went out. Father must have overheard the talk about the bet. "Cancel that bet, children. I wouldn't want your mother to hear of it. But Lucy, you may soon strike it rich. With a new baby you'll have a lot of baby-sitting pay. Even a new boy can be valuable, can't he?"

"I got to tell the boys it's a brother and not another sister." Amory picked up his jacket and started for the door. "Go by way of Kleins' and ask for extra milk tonight," Mrs. Sanderson said.

"For Mother or the baby?" Lucy asked, after Amory had left.

"For the baby. Your mother says she never was a good nurser, and at her age, it's hopeless."

"Good. Then I can feed him." Lucy could see some advantages.

"You've not had a good look at your new son, Mr. Johnston." Mrs. Sanderson moved the basket slightly so that Father could clearly see the wrinkled face.

"He'll do," Father said. "Lucky I've had experience in seeing our others when they were newborn."

"What will you name him?" Mrs. Sanderson asked Father.

"That will be up to Caroline."

"Oh, I know," Lucy spoke up. "She said if it was a girl I could name her Alice, but if it was a boy, she'd name him after you, George Henry Johnston, and we'll call him George."

"Named after me?" Father grinned. "That's news."

"Yes, Mother said it was to be a surprise. After Amory was named for her father, she was sorry your name wasn't used instead."

"So now we've got that corrected, without changing Amory." Father laughed.

"I can't imagine Amory with any other name," Mrs. Sanderson said. "No other boy I know has that name, and there's no other boy like Amory, either." And Father agreed.

"I've got to go down to the bank, and Lucy, your mother is awake and ready for you to give her a kiss. After that, why don't you spread the news at the Owens'?"

Lucy went slowly up the stairs, wondering how she could pretend delight over a boy, but once she was in the room, she had no problem. Everything was tidy and warm, Mother had on a fresh nightgown, her hair was brushed and newly braided, and her eyes were drowsy but not in pain. Lucy flung herself down beside the bed and reached out to Mother. "You're really all right, aren't you, Mother? I wanted a girl but he'll be fun anyway!"

Though *fun* seemed the wrong word after all Mother had been through, she slowly moved her hand to the side of the bed and touched Lucy's cheek. "We'll take care of him together," she said. "Now go out for fresh air, and I'll take a nap."

Lucy tiptoed out of the room, and it wasn't until she was in the kitchen that she realized she hadn't kissed Mother. But sometimes kissing wasn't necessary.

Over at the Owens' everybody gathered around Lucy. "A boy! Splendid!" exclaimed Mr. Owen. Lucy knew that the British liked sons, but she wished he wouldn't be quite so British about an American boy born in an American family that already had a boy.

"Bet your folks are glad it's not another girl," Edward said.

"We saw Dr. Carmer on his way home so everything

is fine, isn't it?" asked Mrs. Owen. "Both the baby and your mother?"

"She's fine—well, awfully tired—the most tired I've ever seen her, even after spring housecleaning." They laughed at that silly comparison.

"Not really funny, though, is it, Lucy?" Mrs. Owen asked seriously.

"No. I saw my mother this noon, too," Lucy began. Then she stopped. What she'd seen of having a baby was more than even Mother had intended her to see, and the Owen girls knew nothing about having a baby. So she kept still.

"What'll you name him?" Gwen asked.

When Lucy answered, "George," Guinevere said, "Oh, after King George V of England. But you're Americans. That's in-cred-ible!"

"It's not that George," Lucy explained. "It's George Henry, after my father and his father, too. Of course my father's called Harry, but his real name is George."

"It's a good, old-fashioned name," Mrs. Owen said.

"What's he look like? All pink and white like a baby doll?" asked Guinevere. "Can we come see him?"

Lucy thought of that red, wizened face, and she was glad she could say, "He's so puny that for a few days he's just for the family. Anyway, right now, he's nothing much to see." Suddenly she felt weary. "Now I must go home to help Mrs. Sanderson," she lied. There wasn't anything for her to do until suppertime, but she didn't want to answer any more questions about the baby or about Mother. This afternoon the Owen girls seemed very young to her, like little children.

That night at supper, the three of them sat at the dining room table, Lucy in Mother's place. She poured

Father's tea, passed him the sugar, and then asked Amory as Mother would have, "Amory, please bring in the pitcher of milk I left on the kitchen table." He brought it to her without a complaint, and before he sat down, he asked, "Anything else you need?"

Father praised him. "I'm glad to see that with a third child in the family, you two will be the big ones and won't needle each other." Lucy opened her mouth to say something about this, but Father went on. "You really are a lucky girl, Lucy. Your mother didn't produce the sister you wanted, but today's mail brought you a sister anyway."

He handed her a pale blue envelope, slit along the top and addressed to Father. "Foreign stamps—it's from France," Lucy said. "Did you write for a French war orphan's name? And did you send some money to help? And—"

"You might take it out and see?" Amory suggested.

Lucy pulled from the envelope a very thin sheet of paper with a few lines of purple writing. With it was a photo of a little fair-haired girl, about five years old. Lucy stared. "A blonde? I thought all French children had brown eyes and black hair. You sure she's French?"

"Of course she is. She lives in Brittany, and in that part of France there are lots of blondes. But what do you think her name is? Turn over the photo and you'll see."

Lucy turned it over and read LUCIE. "Not spelled like my Lucy, but I like it. How did it happen?"

"I asked for a Lucy if that was possible," Father admitted. "It's a name you can pronounce, can't you? Her last name's harder. It's Gailloux, and I think you pronounce it like GUY-YOU. My French is very rusty, but Father Van Mert came into the bank, and he translated the letter for me. It was written by her village priest. 'Madam Gailloux says thank you for the money, and her Lucie sends kisses to her American sister.' "

Lucy was still looking at the picture. "I suppose I'll never really see her, but she's a lot prettier than our new George, that's sure. I'm going to ask Father Van Mert to help me write her a letter. I'll begin, 'Dear little sister' and—"

Father interrupted. "It just goes to show that you do have luck, Lucy. Now you and Amory do the dishes. I'm going to rest on the sofa until Dr. Carmer comes to check on your mother. I'm done in. Having a baby is exhausting at my age." He laughed.

Lucy knew he'd had no sleep the night before and he must be very tired, but her sympathy was with Mother.

The days following the baby's birth were mostly a blur to Lucy. Mother stayed upstairs in bed for two weeks, the doctor came often, and Mrs. Sanderson lived at the house to care for Mother and feed everyone, including the baby. And all the time the baby squalled and squalled. Nobody slept much, and everyone snapped at everyone else—all except Mother, who lay in bed, much of the time lulling the baby, who refused to be lulled.

Two things about the day after George's birth she did remember. The first was Julie Meizner asking her, "Did you cry because there's a new kid in the family, Lucy?"

"No. Why should I cry?" Lucy was puzzled.

"I cried when the last one came at our house. I cried for a whole day and a night. We've already got so many that I just knew I'd have to do all the work for it, like give it the bottle in the middle of the night and change it and keep it quiet and—you know all those things you'll have to do."

"Oh, maybe," Lucy replied. This was something she'd not considered, but it wasn't likely with only one baby. She hoped not.

The other event was that Cyril scooped her with the news of her own baby brother. No sooner was the bell done ringing than Cyril announced, "News! The Johnstons got a new kid."

Then when Mary asked for other news, Lucy remembered something Father had mentioned after he'd been to the station to telegraph relatives about George. "Tom Evans said on the wires there was news about Russia. A revolution, he said, so their Czar's in trouble." Lucy had scooped Cyril on this, but when Mary asked for more about it, Lucy had to say, "Tom doesn't think it's very important. Might not even get into the papers today."

"Well, a new Johnston and a Russian revolution in one day!" Mary said. "And does anybody know about other war news?"

"Guns! Big guns on our ships now and not those candy stripes Germany wanted," Hans Heimle said. "But they've sunk another ship of ours." Hans had seldom talked in school about the news, and when he had, it was always about how Germany would win and never about American ships as "ours."

Only Gwen noticed this shift, and after school she and Lucy discussed it. "If Hans talks about 'our ships,' don't you think all the Germans around here may be changing? Perhaps the spy has stopped working for Germany."

"Would you believe it," Lucy replied, "so much has happened lately that I've almost forgotten the spy."

"I suppose we were dumb even to try that spy hunt. Your father's right, it's only in books that children catch the spy, though—well, sometimes I still daydream about catching him and being a heroine and all that. Silly, isn't it?" Gwen giggled at herself.

"It's in-cred-ible!" Lucy exactly imitated Guinevere's word. Then she went on. "My father was right too about all the changes in 1917, but I didn't think we'd change so fast, did you? I'm a different Lucy in the same skin, still with the same straight red hair and freckles," she ended bitterly.

"Couldn't those change in a turnabout year—I mean with your lucky spell?" Gwen was really a perfect friend.

Whenever Lucy thought of her little Lucie in France, she did feel lucky. So she wrote a brief letter, beginning, "Dear French Sister Lucie," and telling about herself. When she took it to Father Van Mert, Mrs. Ludwig let her in, reached for the letter, and before Lucy knew what was happening, the housekeeper was reading it aloud. "My, my that's a sweet letter, and here comes Father Van Mert. I'll just read it to him too." So she read it a second time, while Father Van Mert stood behind her and grinned at Lucy. Mrs Ludwig then went on and on. "French girl so she must be Catholic, and I wonder if she's old enough for—no, that couldn't be—"

From the back of the house Magic started to caw. "Caw! Caw! Caw!" Lucy could never be sure, but she thought Father Van Mert winked over Mrs. Ludwig's shoulder. "Magic almost never talks now," he said, "just raises a rumpus in his own language." Mrs. Ludwig left them, and the priest promised to translate and mail the note.

War!

AMERICA DECLARED war on Germany on April sixth, a Good Friday. Lucy felt afterwards 'that she should have dramatic memories about such a great event. But it was the early part of the week that stuck in her mind much more clearly.

"April fool! April fool!" Amory yelled through the keyhole of Lucy's bedroom door on Sunday morning. Then he ran down to breakfast.

"I'll fool him! I will! I will!" Lucy said over and over again as she struggled with the knots he'd tied in her long winter underwear, her long stockings, and the shoestrings for her high, laced shoes. After she was unknotted, she hurried down to watch Amory pour on his hot cereal the salt she'd put in the sugar bowl. But at the table Amory was casually eating his oatmeal.

"April fool on you!" He grinned at her. "Salt for sugar is such a hoary old trick that I didn't use the bowl this morning. But Father almost did. I saved you from that!"

Lucy was so shocked at what might have happened, that she almost said thank you. Now and then Amory did stand between her and disaster.

Mother came down, carrying the baby, who hadn't grown and hadn't stopped crying. "Lucy, rock him a little while I try another bottle for him. And Amory, this is Sunday. You save your April fool high jinks for tomorrow."

"Lucy was April-fooling, and not me. It's more fun tomorrow anyway. We boys have something interesting planned—kind of an experiment, you might say."

Mother gave him a keen glance, but her new boy took all her attention. George was less red than he had been, only now he was a dark orange-yellow. Mrs. Sanderson called it jaundice of the newborn and insisted he'd get over it. Yet when the Owens had finally seen him, Guinevere had been too shocked to call him "in-cred-ible," and Gwen had said "Oh, so that's what he looks like. Nice eyes, Lucy." Gwin had really infuriated Lucy by her comment! "You should have seen Edward when he was two weeks old—so beautiful. All pink and white, with golden fuzzy hair."

At school on Monday morning, the hall rang with "April fool!" "April fool!" as everyone celebrated a day late, though once the doors were shut and classes began, the whole school was quiet. Mr. Grady came into Miss Hoffer's room to bring a supply of paper for her and to invite her classes to his room for a science demonstration. He had no sooner spoken the invitation than squeals and screams came from his room, and over them all was a chorus of boys shouting, "APRIL FOOL!"

Mr. Grady dropped the ream of paper so fast that it slithered off the desk and scattered all over the floor. He dashed out of the seventh-eighth grade room, pulled open the door of his high school room and bellowed, "SILENCE!"

Mary Hoffer's pupils jumped up to follow him, paying no attention to her order, "Sit down, all of you. Later we'll go to the science demonstration. Stay here!" Instead they followed Mr. Grady, as they'd been invited to do. But it was not a science demonstration that they saw.

Lucy, because of her front-of-the-room seat, was at the head of the swarm of pupils peering in the door of Mr. Grady's room. There she saw the high school girls standing on their desks, squealing and howling and pulling their long skirts tighter and tighter around their legs. By now all the boys were laughing so hard they could hardly shout April fool. At the side of the room, the two cages of mice were open—and empty.

"Boys!" Mr. Grady commanded. "Get those mice back in their cages—double-quick!"

The April fool shouts stopped, and every boy chased mice. "There's one. Get it for cage number two." "No. He's too skinny. Must be from cage number one." "Two are missing." "One's out in the hall." Now the squeals began among Miss Hoffer's girls, who ran to their room and slammed the door. Lucy was stuck in Mr. Grady's room, unable to push her way through the boys.

"Who did it?" Mr. Grady asked. Lucy tried harder to get away, for she knew Amory must have been a ringleader. "Who did it?" he repeated. The girls had stopped squealing and were in their seats, though they still held their skirts tight.

"Well—you see—I didn't actually do it all. I only sort of helped plan it—as a demonstration about mice and freedom, you could say." Amory stood beside his seat, and he was still spellbinding the whole room as Lucy finally squeezed her way out.

Mary Hoffer was sitting at her desk, waiting for the rest of her pupils. "Mr. Grady knows how to handle any situation. We'll leave the rest of it to him and start on *Hiawatha*." Then Mary, a farm girl who must have seen dozens of mice and even rats in their barn, looked down at her feet, abruptly rose from her chair with a muted "Ohhhh" and moved swiftly to climb a small stepladder near the higher shelves of books.

From the top of the stepladder, she spoke very calmly. "Lenny, please open the door of our room. Harvey and Cyril and Hans, please try to put that wastepaper basket over the mouse under my desk."

The rest of the hour was filled with advice and attempts and failures until finally the mouse was under the basket, a cardboard was slipped under the mouse, the basket put upright and the captive carried back to Mr. Grady's science department.

There were no more calls of April fool that morning, but neither was there much study of *Hiawatha* or cubic feet or the dates of battles.

When Amory came in the door at noon, he asked Mother. "Isn't there something I can do to help? You haven't been up many days, and the doctor says you shouldn't overdo."

Mother paused at the range, stared at Amory, and said, "As the mother of Amory Johnston, I suspect shenanigans. What did you do for April fooling this year? No more chocolate covered soap, I trust?"

"No. I only worked with Mr. Grady's mice today."

Lucy stood looking very wise but not saying a word that might make trouble for him. She sensed he was in enough trouble already. Mother also stood, waiting for Amory to go on. But he had to be prodded. "You worked with the mice? How? You fed them?"

"Well, no. It was kind of an experiment to see if mice that have lived in a cage and fed a lot of good stuff want to get out and run free." He stopped again.

Suddenly Mother understood. "You didn't! You didn't let those mice loose, did you? And they ran all over the school? What will your father say and what—"

"Oh, they didn't run all over the school, only over the upstairs, and it did prove something because—"

"Amory, Amory," Mother said wearily. Then the shed door banged, they heard Father's footsteps in the shed, and Mother thrust the blue water pitcher at Amory. "Go out and pump fresh water—fast as you can. We're almost ready to eat."

Amory ducked out, rushed past Father, and Lucy heard the pump handle squeaking up and down, up and down at a great rate. Mother said nothing to Father about Amory's experiment, and Lucy was handed the bottle to feed the baby in the living room while the others had dinner. Perhaps no one ever told Father about Amory's scientific April fool, but Mr. Grady kept him after school for the rest of the week, cleaning blackboards, cleaning erasers, cleaning windows, but never cleaning the mouse cages.

BECAUSE GOOD FRIDAY was a holy day for Catholics, Father thought it better to have the joint meeting of Boy Scouts and Stone Age Girls on Thursday evening. The boys were to have their final test on knot-tying and the girls were to provide the fudge, though Father agreed they should also have a chance to prove that they now were as good at knots as the boys were.

The girls made the fudge in the afternoon—three large round tins of it. After supper when both clubs were in the dining room, Father cautioned the Scouts, "*Shhhhh*. The baby and his mother are sleeping. And before the fudge, you have to demonstrate your knowledge of knots."

"You said we could show our knowledge too, don't forget," Lucy said. "And if we're good at knots, you'll take us camping."

"Bet you can't tie a tight knot even if you did spend months and months practising," Stan jeered. "Any tent ropes you tied would—"

"All three of you boys sit down and let us take three ropes and show you," Gwen said.

"How much do you bet we can untie your knots in three minutes, maybe in only one?" Amory asked.

"No betting!" Father squelched him. "But let's give the girls a chance. Each of you boys sit in a straight dining room chair, and here are the practise ropes. Guinevere, you and I'll be on the sidelines."

Ordinarily Lucy was clumsy in handling anything, but they'd tied and untied so many knots in their meetings that the task now was almost a trained habit. Around and around and around, with a tight halfhitch and then a firm square knot—all done in little more than a minute. The girls stepped back, Father admired their knots. Then he said, "One, two three. Boys, escape your bondage."

They wriggled and squirmed and lifted their arms slightly, trying to get their elbows free. They tried to get their hands around to the back of the chair, they tried to breathe all the air out of their lungs to make the ropes slacken. Nothing helped, and Father went on counting off the time. "One minute gone. Two minutes gone, twenty-five seconds left, ten seconds left, and the three minutes are up! Girls, you've won!" The girls couldn't be very loud about their victory, but they made the most of it in teasing and mocking the boys.

"Now see how fast you can untie them, girls," Father said. That was the problem. The boys had struggled and pulled on the ropes until not one of the girls could untie them. Father was immediately unhappy. "My good ropes, tied into permanent knots," he grumbled, as he too tried to untie the boys. The three Scouts began to raise a fuss. Father dug at the knots with his penknife, and muttered, "Jumping Jehosophat!" and then, "Rats! Rats! RATS!"

The girls stood aside, looking concerned about their success, the boys began to complain even more loudly, and finally Father said, "Lucy, get the big shears from the shed. Whose blamed idea was this! I've got to cut my best camping ropes and look how your mother's dining room chairs are rubbed right down to bare wood. And whose blamed idea was this?" Lucy handed him the heavy shears, but nobody answered him.

Before long the fudge had soothed the boys, the girls said no more about knots, and Father hunted in the shed for stain to cover the damage to Mother's chairs. Soon Mr. Owen came to take the girls home, staying long enough to tell Father that Congress was still debating a declaration of war.

"By tomorrow, I think America will be in it." Mr. Owen spoke with enthusiasm.

Father had long expected war, but he answered without any excitement. "If not tomorrow, then very soon —and America will never be the same again. Even villages like Wales will change." Lucy heard his words like an echo of the New Year's Eve prophecy for a turnabout year.

"Maybe all the prophecies will come true, even my going away one," she said to herself later. "Anyway, a lot has changed. I'm in the eighth grade, and the baby is here."

At three o'clock in the morning she woke and didn't have to tell herself that the baby was there. Downstairs, Father's bass voice was repeating over and over, "Hushabye, baby, on the treetop." He was obviously walking, carrying George and circling through the three downstairs rooms, his monotonous chant and the crying sometimes loud beneath her and sometimes barely heard.

Thinking of Julie Meizner's responsibilities, Lucy decided that this once she should get up. She put on the red bathrobe that had been Amory's and joined Father. "Should I try to quiet him?" she asked. Poor Father was so tired that he simply handed Lucy the wailing baby, blankets, bottle and all. Lucy felt the bottle. "It's cold now. Could you heat it while I rock him?"

So Father brought the low rocking chair to the warm kitchen, settled Lucy comfortably with a shawl over her legs and the baby in her arms. When the bottle was ready, Lucy took it, held it to her cheek to test it and then miraculously as she put it in the baby's mouth, he began to suck the nipple. "Go on up to bed and tell Mother I'll care for him," Lucy said.

How long she rocked the scrawny little yellow baby she didn't know, but he did eventually fall asleep. She put the bottle on the table and took him to the sofa, where she laid him down, stretched herself beside him, and together they slept until it was light.

Both Mother and Father were full of praise, but for all the next day after that she was so weary and fagged that when Father announced at supper that war was declared, she heard the news in a sleepy daze. "We are at war," she said to herself, but really the baby now seemed more important than the war.

For
Liberty Bonds

FOR EASTER SUNDAY all the Ladies Aid brought their most beautiful houseplants for the front of the church—geraniums, pink begonias, Mother's pots of blue and pink hyacinths, and the one Easter lily that Mrs. Flint's relatives sent her each year from St. Paul. Mother was well enough to walk to church with the family and pump the little organ for the music. Hilda Dickerman had gone to early mass so that she could baby-sit George. She was so used to babies that Lucy felt stupid beside her, in spite of Hilda's being a couple of years younger.

Since it was only the eighth of April, the air was chilly, even though the bare ground proved winter was over. No one wore warm-weather clothes, but every single girl had a new spring hat—that is, every single girl but Lucy. Mother did not believe in new clothes for Easter, "and especially not this year, when we've just gone to war." When Lucy began to argue that war had nothing to do with it, Mother said, "When Mrs. Howe has a sale next month at her new millinery store on Main Street, you'll get your new straw hat."

So Lucy had to be content with admiring all the other hats, and for the sake of the Owens, politely listening to the sermon. Actually Mr. Owen's sermon was clearer and shorter than usual. For the first time, he seemed at home in Wales and with his congregation. When she mentioned this at Sunday dinner, Father suggested, "Perhaps it's because his war is now our war too. Mr. Owen has been an isolated man," explained Father. "He'll change after this."

Yet for her, Lucy felt the war had not changed anything. School continued with the cramming of names and dates and poetry for the state exams, a few robins came, Mother grew stronger, but the baby stayed sickly and very yellow and as homely as when he was born.

About two weeks after Easter, they sat at the supper table, without Amory. "He's late again," Mother said. "We won't wait. I want to eat while the baby's asleep— this once I'd love an uninterrupted meal."

As Father spooned out the helpings of macaroni and cheese, Lucy talked in a low voice. "We've been at war now for almost three weeks, but what are we doing about it? I mean what can we do here in Wales, when the war's still across the ocean?"

"Good heavens, Lucy," Mother said in an agitated whisper. "Thank your lucky stars it is still across the ocean."

"You're right, as usual, Caroline, but I do know what

Lucy means. Only the young men volunteering for the army and navy seem to be doing anything."

"I can't volunteer, and so far the tin foil I've collected is only about as big as a tennis ball. So what can anybody do?"

Then Amory banged the shed door. Mother said, "Lucy, quick, catch him before he wakes the baby." Lucy rushed to the kitchen and met Amory, who was about to yell something. She clapped both her hands over his mouth and cautioned him, "Shhhh! Baby's asleep!"

He winked and tiptoed to the table. That baby was working great changes in the family, but not everything was changed, not Father. "Go wash, and do it so quietly that we won't hear you."

Amory obeyed, shuffled to the kitchen in an exaggerated tiptoe, and washed so silently that the baby slept on. Back at the table, Amory cleaned out the big casserole, chose the biggest apple muffin, helped himself to cold ham, and filled the edges of his plate with watermelon pickles and currant jelly. Then he began a whispered account of his afternoon. "I've been out looking for work."

"You! Looking for work?" Mother was astonished.

"Yes, so I can earn money to loan to the government to help win the war. I've been to the butcher shop to see if I could sell cookies and things that don't have to be carved, and I've been to Lowensteins' to see if they'd hire me at the candy counter, and I asked the druggist if I could fill ice cream cones and learn to mix sodas, and I even thought about the pool hall, but perhaps—"

"No *perhaps*," said Father. "No son of mine will hang around that pool hall, whether it's for the war effort or not."

"Anyway, nobody wanted me until Mrs. Howe in her store with women's stuff said—"

Mother interrupted with a laugh almost loud enough to wake the baby. "You're going to sell hats and dresses, or model them or a corset, maybe?" She and Lucy put their napkins up to their faces to stifle their laughs at the vision of Amory wearing a ribboned hat or a fluttery ruffled dress, or lacing up a corset.

Only Amory remained serious. "Of course, if you want to make fun of my war effort . . ." He sounded abused. "I'm going to sweep out her store and help her put stuff on the top shelves and break up the boxes that things come in and—well, do work."

"It sounds as if Mrs. Howe is putting a bull in a china shop, but I'm proud of you," Father said soberly. "And when you didn't get an edible job, you kept right on—to hats. Good for you!"

"We've been talking about it in school, too," Lucy began. "The USA needs all those millions of dollars, and people are going to loan the cash and get Liberty Bonds. But so far, there's nothing for boys and girls— well, only millionaires' kids can buy bonds." Lucy was unhappy.

"Mr. Grady told us that pretty soon the kids can buy War Savings Stamps at the post office for twenty-five cents a stamp."

"It's not much of a war if twenty-five cent stamps are going to win it," Lucy said doubtfully.

"The plan is to save a whole bookful of stamps, then turn them in on a Liberty Bond. And I'm going to get twenty-five cents for every hour I work for Mrs. Howe, so let me see—that's a dollar fifty, a week, and—"

"Hold on!" Mother halted him. "We'll need a lot of your time in the garden this year. Europe needs food as much as money, so we'll have a huge garden and both of you will have to do twice as much weeding as usual."

"And for the extra work, we'll pay you," Father added.

"Weeding! Ugh!" Lucy made a face. "If I could work at Mrs. Howe's—that would be more like a job."

"Your real job this summer is to help me with the baby."

The baby let out a wail. Mother got up and brought George into the dining room. Lucy felt sorry for him. His crying was always pathetic, as though he didn't want to stay alive. Mother rocked him in her arms, motioned to the fruit Jello on the kitchen table and asked Lucy to bring his bottle also.

"Will he ever be a well baby and a happy one?" Lucy asked, as Mother tried to feed him and he refused to suck, only continued to cry, more a sad complaining than a baby's crying.

Mother tried again with no success. "Here, Lucy, take him to the other room and do keep trying him on his bottle." Then to Father she said, "He's over a month old and hasn't gained an ounce, and he's still the color of an orange. I wish we had a baby specialist nearer than Grand Forks, but Dr. Stewart in Langdon does know a lot about babies. If I took George to him, could you and the two children get along here?"

"You go," Father told her. "There's nothing difficult about housework, and I'll pay the children in War Savings Stamps."

"Fine with me," Lucy called from the living room. Much as she had wanted this baby, she'd be glad for a brief vacation from the sad, wailing infant.

So Mother and the baby went to Langdon on Thursday's train to spend two nights with the Johnston cousins and consult Dr. Stewart. That night Father took apart the base-burner stove in the living room and stored the pieces and the pipes and the asbestos mat in the barn.

Then the Stone Age Girls got their brilliant idea for earning money and helping Mother at the same time. Together they'd do Mother's spring cleaning. They'd "turn out the house," as everyone called spring cleaning. And that was the right term for it. Everything that could be taken outdoors was taken out until every backyard in the village was decorated with lines of curtains and rugs and pillows and mats.

Friday was a holiday for the teachers to go to a county meeting, so early in the day the four girls in their oldest dresses began turning out the house. They moved furniture, they whacked rugs on the clothesline, they climbed on stools and chairs to take down pictures, and they whitened the windows with great swishes of Bon Ami cleanser and then rubbed it off. They shook curtains, they brushed down walls, they washed floors, they dusted books and chairs, and they waxed linoleum. Near noontime, the boys came in for a snack. "Who told you to tear apart our house? It'll never be the same again! And how much are you getting paid?" Amory asked.

"We think we'll get quarters, for the war, you know," Gwin answered.

"We'll help you," Amory at once announced. "Mother would like us to work together, wouldn't she?"

"But we've done the hardest part. We only have to put it in order again," Lucy said.

"You haven't done the kitchen pipes, I'll bet. I helped last night, so I know how to do it, and once a year the folks always take down these pipes to clean out the soot."

"Yah, it's a regular part of spring cleaning," Jerry agreed.

"If we don't clean the pipes, the housecleaning isn't done, and besides—" Amory looked very serious, "if they aren't cleaned, there's a danger of fire."

"He's right," Gwin said. "You can't clean out the soot after the spring housecleaning, can you?"

Lucy was uncertain. "I suppose we should do it, but these pipes are twice as long as the living room ones were." Meantime stools and the stepladder and chairs for the girls were placed under the pipes and Amory was in command.

"I think you begin by the hole into the chimney— or is it in the piece next to the range?" he asked Stan.

"Don't you know? You said you knew how, from last night!" Lucy scolded.

"Maybe you start in the middle," Stan said in a faint voice.

"Who took all the rugs outdoors?" It was Father home for his dinner. "WHO TOOK—" he opened the kitchen door, the boys in their astonishment began to waver in their hold on the middle pipe, Father dropped his bag of groceries, grabbed for the pipe and yelled, "Help me hold this thing. Girls, spread papers over everything and close the door so there's no wind to blow the soot around. And of all the blamed and blasted . . ." Lucy wasn't sure what he did say after that, but she judged by the expressions on the Owen faces that he used words never used at the parsonage.

Then Father slowly angled down the middle section of pipe so that the soot cascaded down to the newspapers and onto nothing else. "Since there's no fire in

the range and no dinner for us, we'll finish the job,"
Father said grimly and went to the shed to put on his
old overalls. Then while the girls looked on helplessly
from the dining room doorway, he and the boys took
down the rest of the sections of straight pipe and carefully lifted them outdoors to dump the year's soot in
the weedpatch. Father complimented himself, "Not
hard, you see, for an expert."

Only the small elbow pipe above the stove refused to
budge. Father gently jiggled it, tugged at it, jerked
harder and harder, until suddenly it split off, bounced
on the stove, and tumbled to the floor, scattering soot
to blacken the whole room.

The girls let out an "Ohhhhh!" The boys, nearly as
black as the room, stood aghast, staring at Father. For
a moment he only scowled at the mess. Then he began
to laugh, and he laughed so hard that they joined in. He
was laughing at himself. "By Jove, done by an expert!"

"Ma's just home from a case in the country," Stan
said, when they finally took a look at themselves and
the sooty kitchen. "I'll bet she could make everything
look like new." And with the help of the girls, that's
exactly what Mrs. Sanderson did before Mother came
home Saturday afternoon.

Amory and Lucy met the train; Mother got off and
Lucy reached for the baby and Amory reached for the
suitcase. "Bring us any presents?" he asked. "And wait
till you see the surprise we've got for you at home."

Mother handed him a yellow baggage ticket. "The
baggageman will give you something for this. Wheel it
back here."

Amory dashed to the open door of the baggage car,
handed up the piece of cardboard, and asked, "Please,

may I have this right away? It must be something for me—maybe a bicycle?"

The man glanced at the check and laughed. "Well, now, I don't believe you'll ride on it much, but if you want it in a hurry, here it is," and from the back of the car he pushed forward a large wicker baby carriage. "Hold out your arms, boy, It's all yours. Use it all you like," the man joked.

"A baby carriage!" Amory said in disgust.

"Oh, Mother, it's brand new!" Lucy exclaimed. "You bought it in Langdon, didn't you?" She put the baby down on the cushion, moved the carriage top to and fro to test it, stepped on the little brake at the side, and went on admiring. "Pale gray corduroy inside and a handle just right for me to push it. When can I take him for a ride?"

"Right now. While I stop for a second to see your father, you wheel the baby toward home. And Amory, you carry the bag. In it is the new baby food. Poor baby, Dr. Stewart says he's been starving on ordinary formula. He'll soon be a well baby. We only have to wait awhile."

"Waiting!" Lucy exclaimed. "I never saw such a baby for making everybody wait."

She pushed him briskly along Main Street, not wanting to show George until he looked more like other people's babies. But before she was past the priest's house, Mrs. Ludwig came running out. "Do let me see that Johnston baby, Lucy. He must be growing so fast, and how nice you can wheel him and I love tiny babies and oh, do let me see him." She could outtalk anyone in town, even Amory, and she stood smack in front of the carriage so Lucy had no choice but to stop.

Mrs. Ludwig leaned over the carriage. "I've wanted

so much to see him. My husband's cousin's name was George—a handsome man. And who does the baby look like?" Then she caught sight of the wizened orange face, and in surprise she couldn't say a word, only "Tut, tut, tut!" and again "Tut, tut, tut!" Finally she started to talk. "Has your mother tried—"

"She's tried everything. Now the Langdon doctor has a new baby food for him. I've got to hurry so we can try it." Lucy drew the blanket over the baby's face and pushed on toward home, leaving Mrs. Ludwig with no one to talk to.

Nearly home, Lucy was passing the Flints' house when Mrs. Flint rapped on the window, and as Lucy paused, both Dorrie and her mother came zooming out their front door. "Lucy, I simply must see that cute little sweetie of a baby," Mrs. Flint cooed. Dorrie reached in and pulled the blanket from the baby's face.

"Mommy! He's yellow! Like those Chinese people in my book." She gazed first at the baby and then up at her mother. "He's not like us, is he? Did Mrs. Johnston get him in China?"

George, as though outraged, let out his usual wailing cry, and Mrs. Flint peered at him, saying, "He is unusual looking, isn't he?" Then she must have remembered her manners. "He won't always have jaundice, Lucy. Someday he may look just like other babies. My Morrie and my Dorrie were the most heavenly little dolls, really like angels. So someday your baby—" She fixed her eyes on George, now squalling himself red as well as yellow, and she added, "Someday, maybe. Come, Dorrie, we must run back in."

Lucy pushed the last block as fast as possible, with Mother by now hurrying behind her and Amory already at the front door. He swung it open. "Welcome home, Mother. All the spring housecleaning's done."

Mother stepped in. "The windows are shining and the base-burner is out for the summer! Who did it?"

"We all worked like dogs," Amory began before Lucy could interrupt. "And those kitchen pipes—were they full of soot!"

Mother stood rooted in the living room. "The stove pipes!"

"Look and see how nice it looks in the kitchen. Mrs. Sanderson helped a little, after the pipes were down."

At the mention of Mrs. Sanderson, Mother found strength to go to the kitchen. It was spotless, and even the range was a polished black with the nickel trim as shiny as Mrs. Flint's stove. Mother's kitchen was the brightest and cleanest it had ever been. "Children, my dear children!" Mother said. And not even Amory asked what they'd be paid.

When Father decided on four times as many war stamps for the girls as for the boys, Amory argued. "But we did the delicate work. Handling those pipes full of soot—isn't that delicate?"

Father began to laugh. "That much I'll admit—very, very delicate!" And he confessed to Mother his part in spring cleaning.

Later, as they finished the chocolate pudding Lucy had made, Mother said, "Listen! Not a peep out of the baby. He took a whole feeding of that new formula and fell sound asleep. Harry, he'll grow to a boy and then a man, after all."

"Give him time, Caroline. Don't be like Lucy—always trying to rush life."

State
Examinations

MAY DAY usually meant May baskets of crepe paper
and lace or ribbon, with colored jelly beans and perhaps one or two crocuses inside. This year to Lucy,
the first of May meant only that the state examinations
were two weeks away. The bigger schools in the state
gave their own exams and final grades, but the village
and country schools must send their eighth grade and
high school pupils to the county seat for a day of writing on questions set by the state board. And Amory
was right—the questions were often tricky.

Mary drilled them on facts and spelling and rules and
dates, on *Hiawatha* and geography and the history of
North Dakota. But she warned them of one question
they must face alone, a brief essay on an opinion of
their own. When they pressed her for ideas, she refused

to help. "It's your opinion and not mine. But do some thinking beforehand," she warned.

Every day Lucy intended to "do some thinking beforehand," but every day had too much else in it, like the Red Cross knitting she was trying to learn. Mother had brought back from Langdon a kit of yarn and instructions for knitting helmets and socks for the soldiers. Lucy's first gray sock had been knitted and ripped and knitted and unraveled until the yarn was worn and frayed. Mrs. Owen could crochet but not knit heels as the Red Cross required them. Mother was left-handed and she used that, plus the baby, for an excuse. Lucy grew more and more discouraged.

"Mother, sometimes I think I won't finish knitting this sock until the war is over," she said as they sat late one afternoon, Mother feeding the baby his new formula.

"Look how he's gaining, Lucy. On such a skinny baby every ounce shows, doesn't it?"

"Uh-huh, but what about this sock? I've dropped another stitch, and if I go back for it, I'll drop three more—and what's wrong with me anyway?"

"Lots of women around here do knit socks, for their men in the fields if not for soldiers," Mother said. "Why not ask Mrs. Schnitzler? She's home for the summer now, and she loves to chat."

"She chats in German, though, Mother, so I'm not sure I'll understand." But Lucy gathered up her unrolled tangle of yarn, and her four steel needles, two empty of stitches, the other two here and there holding a stitch with tiny loops between.

It was only a few steps along the back walk and out the gate to Mrs. Schnitzler's low house in the next yard. When the old lady came to the door, she at once saw the resemblance to a sock in Lucy's hands. "You knit already? Socks for your Pa?"

"No, it's for the Red Cross to give to the soldiers," Lucy explained.

"Yah, yah, but you take out two needles? *Zwei?* Oн, Oн, no, no! *Nein, nein!*" She took the jumble of snarls and needles, sat down in her upholstered rocker, and pulled out rows and rows of knitting. Then like lightning she began to reknit what it had taken Lucy ten days to accomplish.

When it was once again near the heel, she handed it back to Lucy. "For heels, you do *ein, zwei, drei*, over and on and you put and you take, and you'll see—easy!"

Lucy knew this was hopeless. She said her thank yous, pretending she had no more problems, but at home she admitted her sock heel was as much a mystery to her as before.

"We won't tell Mrs. Schnitzler that you need more help, but the Owen girls want to heel socks also. We'll ask Mrs. Bortz if she'll show all four of you. That way we won't hurt Mrs. Schnitzler's feelings. Mrs. Bortz can speak beautiful German, but she uses English, you know, when English is necessary."

So on a Saturday afternoon in May, four girls took their gray knitting to Mrs. Bortz, and not only did she teach them how to heel a sock, but she gave them a party of tall glasses of milk and seven varieties of German sugar cookies. Yet when Lucy's pair of Red Cross socks was completed, she thought Amory might be right. "Feel the knots in the foot of that sock, Lucy. If some soldier does avoid getting wounded in battle, he's going to be permanently crippled anyway—from your knitting."

Real spring had come, and to Lucy this meant taking

off her long winter underwear, hanging her heavy coat and her wool hood at the back of the coat closet, and trying on last year's summer dresses to see how much she'd grown. "Not an inch," she lamented to herself. "And the Owens—even Guinevere is getting taller all the time." Amory had noticed this, and teased her for being the "pipsqueak of the Stone Age Girls," but Mother tried to comfort her, saying, "Size is much more important for boys, so it's Amory and George who must grow."

She wished she were bigger, just as she wished for curly hair like Gwin's; but on a fresh May morning with meadowlarks singing everywhere and with the Owens to meet on the way to school, who could worry about size or state exams or even a war?

But the war was more and more a reality, with talk of drafting young men for the army, talk of the U-boats sinking American ships, and always talk of the need of growing more food, and saving more food and sending more food to starving Europe.

"This is a new recipe for bread to save wheat," Mother explained, as she passed around a plate of soggy gray bread at dinner.

"What's it made of? Last winter's blankets chopped up in dishwater?" Amory asked after one mouthful.

Everybody laughed, but when Mother spoke of oatmeal in it instead of white flour, Lucy groaned loudly.

"No groaning, Lucy. Your little French sister Lucie would be glad to get it." Then in one of the shifts that Father often surprised them with, he asked, "What would you think if I bought a farm, a wheat farm, of course?"

"You're still considering it?" From her mother's

voice Lucy knew that her folks didn't agree on buying land.

"This farm's different, Caroline. It's the one Helge Helgeson rents from that Minneapolis bank, and it's up for sale. Almost five hundred acres of prime crop land, and with this war, the price of wheat will double before long. A farm now can't help but make money."

"You mean we'd still live here and you'd work at the bank and the farm would only be to make money?" asked Amory.

"All the farmers expect to make money, but most of them never do, Harry. Most of them only get bigger mortgages instead of bigger bank accounts. You say that yourself," Mother argued. "And crops are such a gamble—always too dry or too wet or too hot or too cold."

"But this year, with the high prices, and any luck at all, a big crop of wheat is more food for Europe and more cash for us." Father and Mother seldom argued before the children, so Mother didn't answer.

It was Lucy who asked the next question. "Cash? Then you'd have cash to send me away to a big city school?"

"Certainly not until you finish the two years of high school here and—"

Amory interrupted Father. "And pass those state exams!"

"Let Lucy forget those exams for a few hours," Father said. "You might like to know what I heard today about that Wales spy?" He paused to see their instant attention. "When I had no news about anyone here, I wrote that detective and I find he's gone back East, where he belongs, the idiot!"

"But where's the spy?" Lucy almost said "my spy," since he had once been so important to her.

"Not in Wales, but probably in Canada near our border." Then Father grew angry, thinking of the insult to Wales. "They suspected Wales only because of all our German-Americans. Some Canadian who might want or need the money could be guilty. Just see, Lucy, the harm you might have done, going off on a childish spy hunt."

Lucy made no reply. That spy hunt was something she wanted to forget.

WHEN LUCY finally drove down to Langdon with Father and Amory to take the exams, she was in a tizzy. Leaning forward from the back seat, she asked Father, "Do you think I know enough to pass after only about three months in the eighth grade? And Mary's new— would she know how to coach us right?"

"Quit it, Lucy," Amory shut her up. "Here I sit going over Latin conjugations and the kings of England and how many ounces a mouse gains on the right diet."

"On mice, you're an expert," Lucy reminded him, but Father didn't notice her hint. "Even the dates of Columbus I'm forgetting."

"Mary probably told you that Columbus sailed the ocean blue in fourteen hundred ninety-two, but you've got to remember that in fourteen hundred ninety-three, Columbus sailed the deep blue sea."

"In my day," Father began, "we learned that Columbus went sailing more and more until he sank in fourteen hundred ninety-four."

"Stop it! Both of you! You're only teasing, but you could mix me up. Now about feet, yards, and rods—

how many yards in a rod always confuses me." As she said it, Lucy thought of Franz. For a moment she looked out over the wide expanse of flat fields, with the wind-puff white clouds high overhead, in a sky as blue as bright blue paint. "A barn as big as a whole farm-yard," she said to herself. But soon she was back in today's problems.

"If they ask me that problem about a train and an auto both traveling twenty miles an hour, how soon do they meet at the crossing—well, am I the only one that sees a wreck, the engineer and driver both dead?" Lucy didn't expect them to answer that.

Since the Langdon schools had been let out for the day so that the building could be used for the exams, the two younger cousins were at home. "Look at my new bike!" Len yelled, as the auto drew up. And Lucy had to admit it was a beautiful bike, exactly the kind she had dreamed of. Lucy couldn't even ride a bike, since the rough board walks in Wales and the rutted roads would jounce any bike to pieces in no time. But someday she intended to have a girl's bicycle, a white one with a wicker basket strapped to the handle bars and a New Departure coaster brake. "If I go away to school . . ." she said to herself, "and I am going—I'll get a bike!"

"This is a boy's bike, of course, but you could put on my overalls and try it," Len offered.

"Overalls on Lucy! Leonard!" Aunt Effie appeared at the door with Ed, the cousin about Amory's age but far bigger.

"Hey, Amory," Ed yelled. "Glad you got to take those exams, and we get the holiday."

"Yeah, but I'm going away to a military prep school and drill with a gun." Amory always outboasted Ed.

"Go along, Harry, and deliver them at the school. Here's a doughnut for each of them to munch on the way." Aunt Effie's doughnuts, outside toasty brown and sweet inside, were extra special.

So Father drove them to the brown brick school, gave Amory a thump on the back and said, "Do your best and stay out of mischief." Then he kissed Lucy and grinned. "You'll be all right, just don't be a worry-wart."

The building was much bigger than the Wales four room school, but it seemed commonplace compared to the dream school Lucy had in mind. Indoors the oiled floors, the tan walls, the worn stairs were very ordinary. She dreamed of wide halls, marble stairs, tall windows, and an auditorium with velvet curtains and a stage and rows of theater seats and absolutely no desks. The Langdon auditorium was nothing but a large school-room for about a hundred and fifty pupils. There Lucy was handed her exam sheets, and everyone bent over the desks, writing, writing, writing.

At noon she and Amory went to Aunt Effie's for dinner, and though Amory ate enough for both of them, Lucy only sampled her food. The arithmetic and spelling and grammar and geography hadn't been bad, but she still had an afternoon of history, the lines from *Hiawatha* and that essay on her own opinions. She wished it was over and done.

Her older cousin George was home for dinner, and surrounded by the three strapping boys, Lucy looked so tiny that her Uncle Charlie pitied her. "It's all wrong, Harry, for youngsters to face these tests just because they come from small schools."

"What's really bad," Father answered, "is that many are afraid to try and they leave school. Someday Wales,

I hope, will have a bigger school, perhaps even four years of high school." To Lucy this was a new idea, but she kept her mind on *Hiawatha*.

At the end of the afternoon, Lucy felt she'd not disgraced herself, but she did have misgivings about her opinion essay. She said nothing about it except to Gwen the next day. "I did what my father says I should do. I made up my own mind about what the Indians did in that Walhalla massacre, scalping those missionaries. And I'll bet I'm in trouble. You wait and see!"

In ten days, Mary Hoffer had the grades, and she must have spoken at once to Father. At supper, he quizzed Lucy, "What in tarnation did you write in your opinion essay, Lucy?"

"Well," Lucy began as Amory always started his explanations. "Well, you always say I should come to my own decisions, so I wrote that I thought the Indians in the Walhalla massacre weren't as bad as the books say. Scalping was just their way. That's all I—"

"Lucy! You wrote in favor of scalping? Makes you sound like a savage!" Mother exclaimed.

"But look at what the whites did," Lucy argued. "They stole the land and they cheated in the fur trade and they made Indians change their religion. How would we feel if—"

"I do like to have you make up your own mind," Father soothed her. "But must you be so violent about your opinions? Your essay was just like kicking those examiners in the shins."

"Did I flunk that part of the exam?"

"No, but pretty close to it—only a 76."

"That girl's a dummy and a disgrace to the family."

"Keep still, Amory. And Lucy, since you may hear it anyway, I'll tell you that if you hadn't favored scalping, your grades would have been among the top in the county."

"Huh! She must be born lucky—only luck could—"

Father ignored Amory. "Think a little more about scalping, Lucy, before you prescribe it for someone else. If I take all of you camping this summer on the Pembina River, how would you like to have a band of savages jump out of the woods and scalp everybody?"

Lucy never liked to admit defeat in an argument, but she did get a glimmer of Father's point. "I wouldn't like it. You know that. But how about this deciding things for myself? Every single time I make up my own mind, I get into trouble." She wanted to go on and remind him that she'd made up her mind to go away to school in the fall, but she knew that would only land her in more trouble.

Amory began a long recounting of the wages he was earning at Mrs. Howe's shop. Then Father spoke of all the wills he was writing for young men. "The conscription bill is passed now, and all these husky chaps who grew up on farms will be among the first to be drafted, and of course, they know the danger."

"Everything's changing, even Wales, and the young men and their families . . . Oh, Harry, last year seems far off from 1917, doesn't it?"

The Branch Line
and
The Empire Builder

"LUCY, I hear Mrs. Howe's sale of hats begins today. You run down early and get your hat. It's Saturday, and soon a lot of people will be in town."

Each day, on the slightest excuse, Lucy had gone by that store, watching for the SALE sign. Today, sure enough, across both big windows were pasted paper banners: SALE. Already at one window, waiting for the store to open, stood Mrs. Flint and Dorrie, so intent that they didn't even notice Lucy. She moved closer to see that her favorite hat with a blue ribbon and rosebuds wasn't yet sold, and then she gasped.

Mrs. Howe must have hired all three Scouts to help that morning, and there they stood, right inside the windows, each wearing one of the fancy straw hats. Amory wore her chosen one, balanced at a silly angle, while he smirked and stuck out his tongue and jigged a ridiculous dance. The other boys imitated Amory and none of them saw what Lucy saw—Mrs. Howe coming in the back door behind them.

Mrs. Flint now noticed Lucy, and loudly told Dorrie, "It's that awful Johnston boy again, but you just wait. He'll get his comeuppance."

Lucy shook her head violently at Amory to warn him, but he only increased his antics. Then Mrs. Howe picked up the broom and whammed it down on Amory's head and on the hat. Alas, they both got their comeuppance. Amory let out a yell, the straw and the rosebuds flew all over the shop, Stan and Jerry tossed their hats into the air, and all three boys came out the door so fast that Lucy and the Flints were almost catapulted into the air, too. Lucy took off for home at once, leaving the Flints far behind.

"I saw that hat again, Mother," Lucy explained, "and I wouldn't buy it now for a hundred dollars. It isn't what I thought it was." She didn't tattle, but she was curious as to how Amory would get out of this scrape.

At supper, Amory asked Father if there was a chance of a job Saturdays on a farm perhaps. "I think Mrs. Howe doesn't need me any more." Then seeing Mother stare at him suspiciously, he began, "Well—" he paused again. "Well, you see—"

"Get on with it, Amory, and omit your 'wells,'" Father ordered. "What have you done now?"

"It's just that I tried on a hat this morning and I didn't know those silly hats were worth so much money, and well—I didn't ruin the hat, but Mrs. Howe did and she says it's my fault, so I've lost that job and I don't get paid for this week either. And do you think that's fair?"

"Caroline, hats are your province. If he's not telling the truth, Mrs. Howe will probably tell you sometime." But when Lucy thought of what Amory had told them, she saw that actually all he said was the truth, only a lot was left out.

"Now for more important things than ladies' hats." Father was excited. "Today the school board met, and next year the lower grades will need so much space that there'll be no room for any high school, not even the two years they have now."

"No high school? You mean our Lucy, not yet twelve, will have to go away?" Mother sounded as though it were the end of the world.

"Can I go to a big city school after all? Not Langdon, but really big—like Minneapolis? Can I?" Lucy saw her whole life changing and her secret prophecy coming true.

"That's not likely," Father said. "Langdon is near and cheap, and Wales will pay whatever Langdon charges for an out-of-town pupil. When your cousin George goes away to school year after next, your Aunt Effie will have a room for you. For one year I might get state permission to tutor you at home."

"At home? Not in any school? And everybody gone? Awful!" Lucy exclaimed.

"I'd love to have you here," Mother said. "Plenty of time to go away later, and there's the baby to watch, and you'd have a chance to grow and—"

"I'll tell you what I have in mind for your eighth grade graduation present," Father broke in, "and then you won't be so unhappy. Next Tuesday I must go to Minneapolis to sign the papers on that farm. I'm taking Amory so his grandfather can go with him to see Pillsbury Academy, and since you're still half-fare, I've decided to take you too. How does that sound?"

Lucy had heard the trip discussed, but now that she was going, it was a totally different trip. "On the Empire Builder from the Forks all night to Minneapolis? We'll stay at Grandfather Gale's and I'll get to know his new wife, Auntie Kate? And could I get new clothes in the city? How about my looking, only looking, at the high school?"

Father laughed. "Sometimes you run on worse than Amory. Your mother can decide about clothes, but I'll say *yes* to all the rest. Now listen carefully, because it's not a promise. If—you hear that *if?*—if the wheat crop on the farm should be tremendous, it's possible I could make enough cash to pay both Amory's tuition and your expenses for one year of high school in the city. That's why I want you to look at it. Maybe it's not what you want, after all."

"But I know it's what I want!" Then ignoring Father's warning, Lucy pictured herself taking her secret prophecy out of the bank vault and triumphing over everyone. But first, the trip.

On Tuesday the train was so late that when Lucy and Amory carried their bags past the school, the downstairs grades were coming out. "We're coming to wave you off," Gwin shouted, "but we promised to wait until Gwen's out."

"Guess I'll wait until Stan and Jerry are out," Amory announced, putting down his satchel and sitting on it.

Lucy never paused, only called over her shoulder, "What if you miss the train?" Since he didn't answer, she looked back and saw him sitting in the midst of a crowd of younger boys, waiting for the upstairs rooms to be dismissed.

As she hurried past the priest's house, she yelled once

more, "Amory! Come on! Don't stop!" And from the garden came Magic's echoing croak, "Stop! Stop! Stop!"

Father Van Mert came out the back door, laughing. "Magic must remember you saved his life, so he doesn't want you to go away. You're off to the city, I hear."

"I'll soon be back, tell Magic," she said and went straight along to the bank.

At the bank, Father was giving last minute instructions to Mr. Fraser, his assistant, but as he went out the door with Lucy, he noticed Amory was missing. "Is Amory already at the station?"

"He stopped at the school for Jerry and Stan, but he'll make it."

"Make it! He'd better!" Father said ferociously.

At the station platform, Tom Evans was dragging a gray mailbag from his office. "Train made a quick turnaround at Hannah—back before I expected." As he spoke, Lucy looked up the track, saw a cloud of black smoke, and then heard the two long blasts of the whistle at the crossing north of town. With a swish of steam and dust and cinders, the Hannah train pulled in.

No one got off the coach except the conductor. He put down his little stool in front of the three steps, and two women, strangers to Lucy, gave him their bags, lifted their long skirts a few inches and climbed aboard. Next the conductor swung up Lucy's black patent leather suitcase, a Christmas present that she greatly admired, and he helped her climb into the vestibule. There she waited, fearful that she might be the only Johnston to make the trip.

Father went to the edge of the platform and stared down Main Street. "You going?" the conductor asked him.

"Yes, but I've got a boy a couple of blocks away, and he's going too."

"Maybe," the conductor answered. "We're ready to go."

Father looked up at Lucy, looked down the street, looked at the conductor. "Could you please hold this train three minutes more, Mr. Donovan?" he asked, and Lucy distinctly saw Father take a silver coin, a big one, from his trouser pocket and slip it into the conductor's hand. All the time Father stared down Main Street as though he had no idea that his hand was giving money to Mr. Donovan.

Then along Main Street burst a stampede of children, Amory leading the pack and Edward far, far behind, yelling, "Wait for me!"

Panting like a racing dog, Amory leaped to the station platform, tossed his satchel to the vestibule, and in one jump was on the train. From there, he grinned down at the conductor and Father. "How about starting this train? You two coming?"

Lucy ducked into the coach, but even there she could hear Father's bellow. "I've a good mind to leave you home! Just who do you think you are?" Then Father came into the coach, shoving Amory ahead of him. Lucy looked out the grimy window and saw the whole cluster of friends waving hard, and through the double glass she faintly heard, "Have a good time. Come back soon!"

She waved and waved to them, calling, "Good-bye! Good-bye!" though she knew they couldn't hear her now as the train chugged faster and faster away from the platform. Soon the engine whistled at the south crossing, up the road from her own house, where Mother was probably rocking the baby and singing softly. "Mother will always be there to come back to, always," Lucy said to herself. Then she put her faded old straw hat on the shelf above her, got out her copy of *St. Nicholas*, and settled on the stiff maroon plush upholstered seat. Amory and Father took out their books, and the five-hour trip on the branch line began.

The first stop was Dresden. No one got off and no one got on. Next came Langdon, where they stopped extra minutes to take on water from the red wooden railroad tank. As soon as they stopped, Amory stood up. "Guess I'll get off a minute and stretch my legs," he said.

Father didn't even look up from his book. "If you get off this train, I'll pay the conductor to start at once and leave you." Amory didn't reply, only sat down again.

After that, through Easby, Osnabrook, Milton, and on. Lucy knew some of the villages from last summer's drive to the city, but now they all seemed alike, except for two or three that had trees. The conductor called out the name of each town, the train ground to a stop, people got off or people got on, the conductor yelled, "ALL ABOARD," the train whistled and steamed on. And every Main Street resembled the one at home—the same wooden buildings, the dusty road, the hitching posts, and an auto or two drawn up by the station.

By now, the coach buzzed with talking, two babies were crying, three little boys and one little girl ran endlessly up and down the aisle in a game of tag. Lucy gazed out the window, and mile after mile looked so much the same that she wondered if they'd ever get anywhere beyond little unpainted houses, big red barns, pastures of black and white cows, children waving from farmyards, and sometimes a woman shaking a white cloth from a doorway and sometimes a man waving his whip as he rode the harrow over black ploughed land near the tracks.

It was nearly dark when they saw the lights of Grand Forks, the end of the branch line. "Be ready to leave at once," the conductor told Father. "They're holding the Empire Builder for us, but not long."

"Down here our train isn't very important, is it?" Lucy said as they stood at the head of the crowd getting off.

As they scrambled off the train, a little old man in a blue uniform and a red cap reached for Lucy's bag.

"Want me to take it?" he asked. For a moment she thought he was trying to take her precious suitcase from her, so she quickly shifted it to the other hand. Then she realized he wanted to carry it for a tip.

Father smiled at the man and answered for her. "We'll not need a redcap—only going across the platform to catch the night train from the West Coast."

"Run, then," the man urged. "The Empire Builder leaves in four minutes!"

So they ran, swinging their bags and trying not to jostle other folk. In a minute they were beside the glossy train, and at each car door stood a white-coated porter. To the first one, Father held out the tickets, the man glanced at them, and said, "Up ahead, Pullman car number 525, The Yellowstone."

"The Yellowstone?" Lucy panted to Amory as they ran behind Father. "But we're going to Minneapolis."

"All Pullman cars have geography names." Amory didn't have breath enough to laugh at her mistake. The next car had very wide windows; and even running past it, Lucy saw tables with white cloths and shining silver and little vases of flowers and people waited on by men in uniforms. "The dining car!" Amory's breath returned. "Hey, let's eat as soon as we get on. I'm hungry." Father was now short of breath and only shook his head.

In the first small window of the next car was propped a white cardboard with black numerals—525. There the porter said, "Good evening. Just made it, didn't you?" The conductor came down the steps, checked Father's tickets, and the porter carried the bags inside, Amory right behind him. Lucy hesitated.

"Hop on, Lucy," Father ordered. So Lucy hopped

on, into the vestibule and through the open door into the Pullman car. It was like no train coach she could remember. Everything was green—the carpet bright green, the one plush seat near the door a gray green, and on both sides of the aisle from ceiling to floor hung dark green curtains. Once more she stopped, and once more Father urged her on. "Our berths are at the other end."

Just then the train jerked backwards and then forward, as the wheels began to turn. "We made it!" shouted Amory.

"Hush, boy, some people are already in bed," the porter said as Father and Lucy came up to their number, twelve.

"You two children will sleep in the lower berth," Father explained, as the porter drew back the heavy curtains. Lucy saw inside a neat little bed with its own pillows and sheets and blankets, and even its own small light. The shade was drawn at the window, and beside it hung a very small hammock.

Father saw Lucy staring at it. "That's to hold your clothes when you undress. Not for you to sleep in."

"Maybe she could, though, and I'd have more room," Amory suggested. Father went up the little ladder to the upper berth, after showing them how to stow their clothes, reminding Lucy not to shut her finger in the washroom door this time and not to call the porter.

"You press that button," Father warned them, "and the porter has to come. He'll be mad as the dickens if it's just for you two."

When they'd gone to bed, Lucy soon found that sleeping with Amory wasn't really sleeping. He suddenly became the size of a giant. He spread out his arms, his legs multiplied and were all over her, and he took so much blanket and sheet that she had to stay awake to fight for any covering.

In the berth above her, Father snored loudly. The train wheels went *clickety-click, clickety-click*, racing over the rails. Most towns they roared through. The train whistled for a crossing, then for a station, there was a flash of light, then the train tore on through the dark. Lucy lifted the window shade ever so little and sat leaning aginst the fat pillow, looking out.

A full moon came from behind a cloud, and she saw that the fields were not so flat as the prairie at home, and the farmyards had a few trees. It was the same Minnesota countryside she'd seen last summer, but from a rushing train every village and farm now looked like a picture of itself and not the real place.

Then coming to a larger town, the train whistled and halted. Lucy could hear muffled voices of people on the platform, and she craned to read the sign BRECKEN-RIDGE. Someone came into the car with the porter and rubbed the curtains as they went by. Amory woke. "What big place is this?" He leaned beside her to look out.

"It's Breckenridge," she told him and felt very superior. "I've been awake all the time."

"So have I." Amory said.

"You've been sound asleep, rolled up in all the covers, too."

"I was only pretending," he insisted.

"That's a fib!" Lucy contradicted. Their voices grew louder and louder. Father leaned down from his berth, opened the curtains and accidentally put his hand on the porter's bell button.

"Look what you've done!" Amory scolded. Father

stuck his head between the curtains to see, and in a moment the porter was beside him, looking in also.

"Your kids playing tricks?" he asked Father. Amory began to answer, then shut up. Father and the porter both withdrew their heads, and Lucy knew extra silver coins would again be passed out. What an expensive trip!

After that, Amory was put in the top berth, Father crawled in beside Lucy, and everyone slept until the porter called them. "It's nearly St. Cloud now. You've time to get breakfast in the diner before Minneapolis."

That woke Amory at once. "Breakfast! Come on!"

Lucy dressed as fast as she could. "Do you think in the diner I should wear my hat? It's my last year's one."

Father smiled. "If you were ten years older, perhaps. But you're still half-fare, so let your red hair be enough."

Few people were in the diner, so they easily found an empty table next to a window. There Amory ordered two of everything, but Lucy could eat only a little of her scrambled eggs.

After St. Cloud, the train went through more wooded land, the towns were more frequent, and before long the conductor called, "Minneapolis!"

A Look
at the Future

THE MINNEAPOLIS STATION had more platforms
and tracks and waiting trains and waiting people than
Lucy had ever imagined. She stuck close to Father and
heard him tell Amory, "When you come down here in
September, I can't be with you, so remember every
single thing about how this trip goes. You'll be on your
own." To Lucy that sounded grim, but Amory only
dashed ahead toward Grandfather Gale, standing at the
barrier. He was in his black suit, waving his black hat
to them and looking very important with his white hair
and white clipped moustache.

Beside him stood Auntie Kate, his new wife. She was
not much taller than Lucy, but much wider, and her
full skirt and full coat made her look even wider than
she was. When they had all greeted each other, Lucy

decided that Auntie Kate looked as if she must be fun, but Grandfather did all the talking. Immediately he arranged the two days ahead.

"Harry, I know you'll be at the bank and the lawyer's both days, and I'm taking Amory on the noon train to Owatonna. He can see the academy today, and tomorrow the principal can see him. He may still have a chance for a scholarship. We'll be back tomorrow night and meet you in time to catch your night train home." He gave Auntie Kate a kiss, and he and Amory strode off, Amory stretching his legs to keep up.

"Alike as two peas in a pod, those two," Father said as he watched them go, "though you have to be with them awhile to see it. They're planners and talkers and born optimists, aren't they?"

As he said it, Lucy knew she was not a planner or a talker, but she did feel she might be an optimist, especially when it came to her prophecy.

Once Father had left them, Auntie Kate talked and planned. "Your Aunt Frances has taken your Cousin Gale away this week for the Decoration Day holiday, so she's not here to shop with you. But she's made me a list of what you'll need if you do come here to school in the fall." She looked Lucy up and down. "You can see I'm not a stylish woman myself, but I'm sure low shoes—oxfords—are what the girls wear."

Lucy glanced down sheepishly at her high black shoes and black ribbed stockings. "What you're wearing is all right," Auntie Kate comforted her, "but tomorrow you and I are going to Central High School, and you might feel less shy if you dressed more like the hundreds and hundreds of other girls."

"Hundreds and hundreds of girls?" Lucy echoed. She knew it was a very big city school, but in Wales

Mother and Father had only spoken vaguely of its size. "And hundreds and hundreds of boys too, I suppose?"

"Yes, indeed. Over twenty-five hundred students now, and pushing three thousand."

"Pushing three thousand!" Lucy gasped.

"You'll know only a few," Auntie Kate told her, "at first, only those in your homeroom." This was a new term to Lucy, although she guessed what it meant.

Now they were walking toward the shopping district, and on the crowded streets, Lucy noticed how many young men were in khaki wool uniforms, the tunics buttoned up high around their necks, the pants rather baggy in the seat, and their puttee strips of khaki wound in spirals from ankle to knee. And now for the first time she also saw sailors in dark blue middies with pants that had buttons across the front, just as the posters showed them. The sailors all wore white duck hats at odd angles. Somehow they all looked ready for fun, and the soldiers looked ready for war and battles.

"This is Donaldson's, biggest department store in the city," Auntie Kate said, moving through the revolving doors. Lucy followed, but as the door pushed her in, she resented it. At Lowensteins' general store, you opened the door yourself, walked in and closed the door behind you. You managed your own entrance, with no whirling. Inside the store, she faced the escalator, something she knew about but had never seen. Beside it was a large warning: DO NOT SIT ON THE STAIRS.

"Who'd want to?" Lucy asked, and when Auntie Kate laughed with her, Lucy began to feel at home, though stepping off the escalator was much like revolving in the door. The moving stairs took charge of her instead of the other way around.

On the third floor Lucy was quickly fitted with low

brown shoes, but her black ribbed stockings now looked worse than ever.

"Thin lisle stockings are what she should have—tan or brown," said the tall saleswoman, who was made taller by a hairdo that rose several inches above her forehead. "Awfully small feet that girl has, and you say she's ready for high school?"

"She's ahead for her age—skipped a couple of grades," Auntie Kate explained.

The woman brought lisle stockings. "Me, I never believed in having children skip."

"Too late to change now," Auntie Kate told her. "The girl's head is ready for high school. All you and I have to do is get her feet ready." Lucy laughed and so did Auntie Kate, but the woman only sniffed and went to the next customer.

"What do I wear to keep these thin stockings up?" Lucy still sat in the shoe department and dangled a pair of the hose in front of Auntie Kate.

"Of course. You don't want to undress and have the high school girls see you're still wearing a child's suspender garters, do you?"

"In high school I undress?"

"You'll undress for gym," Auntie Kate said matter-of-factly. If Lucy had seen the word in print, she wouldn't have been puzzled; but spoken, it sounded like "Jim." She must have looked stupid, for Auntie Kate at once said, "For gymnasium, I should have said. You'll change in the locker room and put on your gym clothes."

"Oh," was Lucy's reply, determined not to show surprise at anything more.

"Aunt Frances said you'd need a Ferris waist." About this Lucy kept still, following her new decision.

She knew it could have nothing to do with a Ferris wheel, but that was the only way she'd heard the word used before.

By the time they'd bought the corsetlike waist, and a raincoat—something Lucy had never owned—Auntie Kate suggested they take a taxi home. "I seldom use one, but we're both tired," she said, as she hailed a taxicab. Lucy felt totally a city girl as she leaned back on the seat and watched the city go by. Wales? Main Street? The Edge of Nowhere? They were hundreds of miles away.

Lucy had not seen Grandfather's city house since she was too young to remember. Now they stopped before a large brown wooden house, with a porch around the whole front, and behind the house, she caught a glimpse of another slightly smaller building with a little cupola on it. In the house they made a downstairs circuit—a big hall, a parlor, a sitting room, the back library—bedroom, through the kitchen to say hello to the maid, Christine, then through the dining room with a broad stained glass window over the sideboard, and finally out to the hall again and up the wide oak staircase to the landing with another stained glass window. All Lucy could think of was the contrast to her house in Wales. "Our whole downstairs could fit in the sitting room," she told herself, as she went on up and counted six bedrooms.

Auntie Kate was right beside her. "This small back room will be yours if you do come to school in Minneapolis, so we're having you try it for this visit. And that's the door to the top floor, mostly attic, but bedrooms too, and here are the back stairs, if you want to go down that way." Luckily the phone rang, and Lucy was left alone. She was positively dizzy from space. She washed, tried on her new clothes, then took them off again, put her old ones on, and went down the back stairs to the kitchen.

"Haven't grown much since you were at Lake Minnetonka last summer, have you?" Christine smiled at her.

"No, but we think I'll get to five feet, and Amory says if I do that, I'll be human."

"That Amory! He's going to the Baptist academy that Pillsbury's endowed, isn't he? I can't imagine that boy in a church school." Christine shook her head.

"Father says it will change Amory, but Mother says Amory may change the church." Christine laughed.

"What's that building?" Lucy asked, looking out the back door.

"It's the old stable. When your mother was a girl, the horses and the carriage and the sleigh and the girls' pony and cart were all in it. And Leonard the coachman lived in the two corner rooms. It's not used now, but your mother might like to have you see it."

Lucy went out, opened the small door and stepped into the stable. Always when Mother told stories about her girlhood, this stable had impressed Lucy as much as the house—not a livery stable like George Henderson's in Wales and not a barn, but a stable that belonged to one family. Now it was swept and bare. She tried to imagine that she smelled hay and harness leather, but it was only an empty building that belonged to the past. Nowadays Grandfather couldn't afford even one small auto to put in it.

She was coming out the door to return to the kitchen when a thin blond boy of about fourteen almost ran into her as he trundled a bike into the stable. "Hello, I'm Ben Larson and I live next door and we've no place to store my bike, so Mr. Gale lets me keep it here."

"It's a nice bike. I like white ones." Lucy wished she were wearing some of her new clothes.

"It's my sister's, but she doesn't want it any more so I'm using it until fall. Then I'll have enough money to buy a boy's model. I sell papers." He watched her as she stroked the handle bars. "You interested in buying it after I get mine? You're the girl who might come to the Gales' for high school, aren't you?" He leaned it toward her. "Here hop on and give it a try."

Lucy was flattered that he thought she could buy a bike, and she liked his not remarking on her small size, but she had to tell him the truth, babyish as it sounded. "I'm sorry, but I can't ride a bike." The boy stared. "I live in a little village that doesn't have concrete side-walks or smooth roads. But if I do come to live here, maybe my father would buy me your sister's bike—maybe."

"Tell you what I'll do." He began a selling speech very much as Amory would have done. "I'll throw in bike riding lessons if you buy it. You come to Minne-apolis to high school and—well, is it a deal?"

"It's a deal," Lucy replied, thinking that Father might have his own ideas on this extra expense. Then carried away by her enthusiasm for both boy and bike, she promised, "Don't sell it to anybody else, and when I come I'll buy it." This satisfied him.

The next morning after breakfast, Auntie Kate put on a light linen coat and anchored her hat with three hatpins. Lucy had neither a linen coat nor hatpins, but she was wearing her new clothes. Only her Wales hat was old. Auntie Kate said, "You look splendid, Lucy. But maybe you should leave your hat here. You won't see any girls on the street at this season with hats."

And when they were on the way to the streetcar, Lucy saw how silly she'd look in a hat, old or that new one in Mrs. Howe's store. She blessed Amory for sparing her that.

They walked briskly the few blocks to Fourth Avenue, waited for the streetcar, and when they got on, Auntie Kate had Lucy deposit fares, "just for practice." The long yellow car went swiftly along the tracks, stopped every couple of blocks as people got on and others pulled a cord overhead and went forward to get off. "All this is exactly what you'll do every day if you come to Central High. Not difficult, is it?"

"No, Auntie Kate, but it's a lot different from going to school in Wales, or even in Langdon. I've counted, and we've gone at least fifteen blocks—why, in Wales we'd be partway to Nordsmiths' farm." Auntie Kate nodded and stood up.

"There it is now. You signal, and we'll get off." Lucy pulled the cord, as though she'd ridden streetcars every day in Wales, and they stepped out in front of Central High School. It was a monster of a building, pale red brick with white stone trimming and white stone porch and huge triple front doors. Since the students were already in classes, Auntie Kate and Lucy went along the broad sidewalk and up the wide marble stairs and through a massive door alone.

Inside, gongs rang, one class hour was over, students streamed into the hall, droves of them, talking and laughing and almost knocking over Lucy and Auntie Kate. "Pushing three thousand, you said, and really pushing, aren't they?" Lucy remarked, but Auntie Kate didn't hear her over the racket.

Until recently, Auntie Kate had been Miss Kidder, an English teacher at Central High, so she went directly

to the principal's office. There she introduced Lucy and explained her errand. The principal had a very scrubbed, just out of the bathtub look. Everything about him was shiny, from his glasses and his polished fingernails to the watch chain across his vest.

To make conversation with Lucy, he asked her, "This high school must be somewhat larger than the school you come from?"

"Somewhat!" Lucy laughed. "We have four rooms and about ninety children in the whole school. Only nine or ten of us will graduate from the eighth grade next month."

"She's got her final grades already," Auntie Kate said. "They're very, very good, excellent, in fact. State examinations, too."

"One wasn't too good." Lucy thought she should be honest. "I got only 76 on my personal opinion essay."

"How could you be graded down for a personal opinion?" he asked.

"The examiners thought mine was too personal, perhaps. I wrote against missionaries. They got scalped, I think, in that Walhalla massacre because the Indians had a religion of their own and didn't want to be preached at, not by whites, anyway—so—"

For a moment both Auntie Kate and the principal looked startled. Then they both burst out laughing, and the principal turned to Auntie Kate. "She certainly can enter Central High in the fall with her grades, but—" he said to Lucy, "no scalping." He shook his finger.

"She's really a mild character," Auntie Kate assured him. "Now if you were going to have her brother!" Then Auntie Kate got up, and they went to see more of the building, which covered two large city blocks.

More students than ever crowded the halls. "Lunchtime for the earliest shift," Auntie Kate explained. "We'll follow and look into the cafeteria. We won't eat here today, of course, but next year you may. Then it will seem like home."

The glimpse of cafeteria was not exactly homelike. The lines were long, the students weren't shouting, but they were talking in their loudest voices. The list of food over the counter was complicated, and yet everyone was told to "Move along quickly, move along." Lucy was glad to leave it and go to see the auditorium. That was perfect. Empty at this hour, it looked enormous, and not only was there a stage curtain of red velvet, but red velvet drapes framed the long windows. The seats were theater seats, and there wasn't a desk in sight.

Finally, the gymnasium—a barn of a room, huge and bare, with a few girls in dark blue bloomer suits throwing basketballs. Since Lucy had no knack with any kind of ball, she watched some girls climbing thick ropes, like monkeys racing for the ceiling. "I could practice that at home," she decided, "and perhaps my sport could be rope climbing, if that's a sport."

Later as they stood at the curb, waiting for a streetcar, Lucy had her first doubts about going to a city school. The day was now boiling hot, a car rumbled toward them, mobs of girls and boys poured out of the school, calling to waiting clumps of friends, and everyone knew everyone else. Only she was out of place.

"You'll get used to it, Lucy. In no time, you'll be an old hand. And look, there across the street is a big

library—all the books you can read." Lucy had already confessed that at home she read and reread the
same books until she was sick of them. A library—even
Langdon didn't have a real library. And she began to
dream of books, and books, and books.

Late that afternoon Grandfather phoned to say that
he and Amory were back in the city, but instead of
coming home, they'd go to a movie with a vaudeville
show. Yes, he knew the Empire Builder left at 10 P.M.
and yes, he and Amory would be there.

Father was upset, since he liked to have Amory
"lassoed," as he said; he hoped they'd make it. And
they did. At the very last moment, when Father was
having ten fits and the long train had pulled in, Grandfather and Amory rushed up.

"What a movie! A wild west one with horses and
badmen and—lots better than *The Birth of a Nation*
that we saw in Wales. And with it, right on the stage,
was a dancer and a funnyman and two jugglers and—"

"Thank you for everything," Father broke in. "You
were good, Kate, to take Lucy around; and Amory,
you get on that train, and did you two get to see the
Academy?" Father was both joking and impatient, as
he climbed to the vestibule beside Lucy and Amory.

"We did, indeed we did," Grandfather called up to
them as the train began to move. "They said they'd
never seen a boy so good in history and on the rifle
range, too."

That night Amory told Lucy the whole story of the
show he'd seen, but when she asked if he'd get a
scholarship, he said, "Only if someone doesn't use his.
But I'm lucky!"

Always in June

Like all trips repeating what was covered before, the journey home was fast and almost dull. Mother was at the station with the baby sound asleep in his carriage. But everyone talked so much at the same time that the baby woke. He opened his eyes, and instead of crying, he smiled. "Mother, he smiled at me!" Lucy exclaimed as she hung over the baby. "He actually smiled! He's a person now, isn't he?" Then Mother smiled too, and Lucy felt the warm family love around her. "I suppose when I go away, that's what I'll miss," she decided. "But I want to go."

That evening they all drove out to the new farm, where Lucy and Mother visited with Mrs. Helgeson and the two girls, one near Lucy's age, while Father went off to admire the starting crops and Amory and the Helgeson boy counted gophers. On the way home Father was so pleased about finally owning a farm that he kept repeating, "It's a humdinger of a farm, and it will have a humdinger of a wheat crop!" After the third time, he stopped praising his property and began to sing "Glory, Glory, Hallelujah," and they all joined in the chorus.

The first day of June there was a knock at the back door before school. Lucy went, and Hilda Dickerman ran in. "I might not go to school today so I wanted to tell you our baby came a couple of hours ago and it's a girl. Almost always in June Ma gets a baby, and this time I've got a sister!"

For a moment Lucy wanted to scream at her, "How come you folks got the girl, and we got the boy?"

But before Lucy could say anything, Mother was talking. "Splendid, Hilda. So now your mother has two girls and three boys. What will you name her?"

"Ma says I can name her," Hilda said to Lucy, "just the way you were going to name George if he'd been a girl. So I'm going to choose the name you liked, and it's in that poem too—Alice." Hilda rushed out, calling back, "I got to watch over Charlie."

"So it will be Alice Dickerman instead of Alice Johnston," Lucy said dolefully to Mother. "But anyway I'm glad George isn't yellow now. I never told you, but Dorrie Flint thought he was from China. I suppose she meant adopted."

"Adopting is one of the best ways to have babies, Lucy. And it would have been a lot easier for me if he had been adopted," Mother told her.

"Yes, I know. I've decided to adopt my babies and not have them the way you did."

"Just think of George as he is now and forget the

day he was born, my dear. I should tell you that a mother quickly forgets the hard part of having a baby and remembers only the pleasure of seeing him after he's born."

"Maybe I'll forget that day too, Mother, but I didn't get much pleasure out of seeing him then. Did you really look at him?"

George began crying in the other room. "There, you've hurt his feelings, Lucy. I'll go flatter him a little, and you run to school."

For the eighth grade and Mr. Grady's room, June was a time of preparation for graduation exercises. Because there would be no more high school classes, one girl and one boy from the ninth and tenth grades were to speak. Sarah Lowenstein and Amory had been chosen. Most of the program, however, belonged to the eighth grade. Everyone had a part—that is everyone whom Mary could persuade to make up a class will or a class history or a class poem. Because Amory was already on the program and Lucy had been so short a time in the eighth grade, Mary and the folks decided Lucy should be a silent member of the class, a decision she liked. So long as she had a new white dress and sat on the stage with the others, she was content.

Not only was graduation a yearly June event, but this year more than ever June was a wedding month, and the Stone Age Girls spent hours in their stone house discussing weddings. Not until the folks talked of the draft registration on June fifth did Lucy realize that some of those weddings were to keep men out of the army.

Amory realized this long before Lucy. At dinner one noon he relayed the score on weddings that he and the Scouts had been keeping. "Just this week, here and in Mt. Carmel, there'll be nine weddings," he said between bites of rhubarb pie. "And we boys think every girl who couldn't get a man before is chasing him now. And the dumb men get married, and we think they're crazy. The army would be a lot better, so why do they do it?"

"You sound like a wise guy, Amory, but perhaps these men aren't very wise either," Father said. "Of course, a married man has more chance of not being called up for service, but he can't be sure, especially if the war keeps on for a long time."

"Goodness, there's always something more this war is doing to men, isn't there?" Mother said. "Think of all the unhappiness in some of those marriages, and one or the other will always feel trapped."

"We boys say Mary Hoffer is trying to trap that Canadian Toby Mitchell, but we're betting he won't ask her. The draft is only for Americans, so your old Mary will be out of luck, Lucy. He's got no reason to get married." Amory was very definite.

"Is Mary going around with that young man who works in the pool hall? You said he was a no-good, didn't you, Harry?"

Father was thinking of something else, so Amory went on. "She's awful anxious to get married, we think. Tim Hoffer's marrying Miss Baxter as soon as school is out and Mr. Grady and Mrs. O'Neil are getting hitched soon, so Mary's on the prowl."

"Amory, what kind of talk is this? And don't forget that Mary is Lucy's teacher." Father was back in the conversation. "And as for Toby Mitchell, he's a hard drinker and hangs around the blind pig far too much. If Mary is interested in him, it may only be because he's new in Wales."

"I've never seen the young man," Mother went on, "but if she perhaps thinks she could cure his drinking, she might—"

"Mary's not the kind of fool who thinks she can cure a man's bad habits by marrying him," Father said. "She's level-headed."

"But you said Lily Morgan was reforming Danny," Lucy reminded him.

"Lucy, my girl, don't you get ideas about marrying to cure a drunkard. Toby is one you've never laid eyes on, either. Now let's forget weddings, except the Scheldt-Baumgarten one. Your mother has promised to play the organ at the Mt. Carmel church for that, and you and Amory are invited too."

"Count me out! I'll baby-sit so you can go, and how many war stamps will I get?" Amory already had almost enough stamps to buy a bond.

That afternoon Lucy and Gwen stayed after school to help Mary, and as they were leaving, Mary asked Gwen, "Did you get that map from your father— the one that has all the battle lines?"

"I forgot, Miss Hoffer, and as soon as I get home we're going to Hannah for the weekend. But if Lucy comes with me, she can bring it right back to you."

The two girls left together, and as they rushed down the stairs, they almost bumped into a young man coming in. "Had to stay after?" He grinned, but Lucy detected an odd slur. He made "stay" sound like "shtay." She also noticed he had big brown eyes and very red cheeks and he wore a pure white silk shirt. His flat straw hat with a red and blue hatband was tilted jauntily.

On the way to the parsonage, the girls decided two things—he must be Toby Mitchell and he was very handsome. When Lucy went back into the quiet building, the door of Mary's room was shut. Lucy paused, then tapped softly on the door. The man was talking louder than the tap. "Don't be an old schoolteacher!"

Lucy knocked harder. Again his voice was louder than the knock. "Why not? You like me, don't you?"

The third time Lucy knocked, she also turned the doorknob and took one step in. Then she wished she hadn't. They both had their backs to her, Mary standing on top of the little stepladder. Toby was reaching up toward her. Just as his arms encircled her legs, she gave a kick and he fell over onto the floor, pulling Mary and the stepladder down with him. Mary was up in an instant. "Don't you ever come here again when you've been drinking," Mary said in a voice Lucy had never heard before.

Then she noticed Lucy in the doorway, and she was quicker than Lucy to recover. "Oh, you've brought the map. Thank you." Then to Toby Mitchell she said firmly, "Please go now. I've a pupil here."

Toby got up from the floor, dusted off his suit, and picked up his hat from the desk. As he did so, Lucy clearly saw his crushed forefinger. Toby Mitchell was the mystery man, the detective's driver.

As she stared, he went out, and he wasn't smiling. Lucy heard him go slowly down the stairs, and the school door slammed shut.

She was just about to follow him out when Mary spoke. "Let's sit down a moment." Then instead of sitting in her teacher's straight chair at her desk, Mary sat down in the seat across the aisle from Lucy's usual place. She motioned for Lucy to sit down, so that they faced each other across the narrow space. Sitting now in an eighth grader's seat, Mary seemed no bigger and not much older than the eighth grade girls.

"I'm sorry about this, Lucy. Of course, there's nothing really wrong about it, but I think I'd rather you didn't say anything about it except to your folks— to your mother, perhaps?"

"Oh, my mother knows about it already— not what just happened now, but about you and Toby."

"What does she know? Is the whole village talking about Toby and me?" Mary answered herself. "Of course, in a small town everybody knows everything about everybody else. But I'm sure your mother wasn't gossiping about me."

"No, she's just afraid you might marry him to cure his—"

"His drinking?" Mary asked. "I go out with a young man a few times and even your folks think I'll marry him?"

"My father says you're too level-headed for that, Mary—I mean Miss Hoffer." Then having gone this far, Lucy blurted out the rest of Father's comment. "He hangs around the blind pig too much."

Mary sat flipping up and down the metal cover on the inkwell at the desk in front of her until at last she stood up. "I didn't mean to have you repeat what you heard at home, but since you've done so, tell your mother everything. And she needn't worry. I'm not going to marry Toby." Mary looked down at Lucy and added almost jokingly, "As a matter of fact, he'll never ask me to marry him."

Before Lucy knew it, out of her mouth came Amory's words. "That's just what the Boy Scouts say about Toby— that he'll never ask you."

"The Boy Scouts?" Mary looked so baffled that Lucy quickly said good-bye and ran for the door and home. Later when she talked to Mother, she omitted Toby's pinched finger and her suspicions. Mother would tease her about being Mrs. Sherlock Holmes and warn her about getting into spy hunt trouble again.

It was like Amory that when the mid-June graduation came, he talked from the platform not once but twice. By now Father was the Four-Minute Man for Wales, one of the thousands all over the USA who spoke at every public occasion to sell Liberty Bonds. He had already done it two or three times, and Lucy admired his short, serious speech. The evening of graduation, however, Father suddenly developed laryngitis, his voice only a whisper.

Too late to ask anyone else to substitute, Father hoarsely suggested to Mother, "I'm not sick, but Amory will have to read my speech." Mother smiled and nodded, as though she couldn't speak either, and Amory was delighted. He folded and stuck in his pants pocket the paper with the few typed lines.

When they were all dressed in their best, Amory in his new tweed knickerbockers and Lucy in a white dress with a sash tied at the new "dropped waistline," they went together to Fischer's Hall. The crowd filled every row of folding chairs since everybody was related to everybody else and everyone had someone graduating. Lucy and Amory went up to sit with the graduates on the stage, Lucy with her feet dangling several inches off the floor, and Amory looking very young, especially beside the boys already in long trousers.

After the "Star-Spangled Banner," came the speech by the Four-Minute Man. To everyone's surprise, Amory came forward. As he did so, he put his hand in his pocket to pull something out. Only the Johnstons were amazed when his hand came out empty. He'd obviously left Father's speech at home, in his other pants. But Amory wasn't fazed. He launched right into his own speech.

"I come to you tonight as a Four-Minute Boy, substituting for a Four-Minute Man with laryngitis. Because I'm a boy, I ask you to buy a lot of bonds so when all of us boys and girls grow up, there won't be any war. And bonds are a good buy, too. I'm putting my money in them, and I know a good thing when I see it." Here he had to stop while everyone laughed and clapped. Then he ended very dramatically. "Buy Liberty Bonds to make the world safe for democracy and for your kids."

The applause was far louder and longer than any Father had ever received. Lucy sat up very straight and clapped hard. She was proud to be Amory's sister.

Next came the "Welcome Song." "We welcome you, we truly do," it began, and every line rhymed with *you*, since the class had decided that *you* was a welcoming word. After the class will and the class poem and the class prophecy, they sang the class song. "We're the class of seventeen, the class that always will be seen, honoring the pink and green, every triumph we shall glean."

That went on for six verses. Then after Sarah Lowenstein read a long essay on the Statue of Liberty, Amory came forward to read his biography of Daniel Boone. Since he'd insisted he was old enough to do this essay alone, Father hadn't even made suggestions and Mr. Grady also kept hands off.

Amory began with a question, which he asked so

provocatively that even Lucy wanted to hear the answer. "Do you know why Daniel Boone never went to school more than a few days in his whole life?" At once, Amory had the whole audience listening. "I'll tell you why. Daniel and the other boys discovered their schoolmaster had a bottle of whisky hidden in the woods. So they poured out the whisky and filled the bottle with an emetic— you know, stuff that makes you vomit, go *awrk-awrk*."

By now the audience was roaring with laughter. When they'd quieted, Amory continued. "Well, when that teacher finally came back in the schoolroom he was awful white and shaky, but he picked up his whip, and he beat every boy in the class because he didn't know which one did it, and he didn't want to miss anybody. So Daniel Boone never went back to school, and when he grew up he went farther than any other explorer on the frontier. It just goes to show how far you can go without schooling."

Amory grinned and waited for the cheers he knew he'd get. Hardly a man there had been as far as the eighth grade, and many of them agreed with the man who yelled above the clapping, "Sixth grade's enough for anybody! Right you are, boy!"

After the rest of the essay, Amory went to his seat with more loud applause, though Mr. Grady, also on the platform, looked taken aback. Even with its last paragraphs on Boone's exploits, Amory's speech was hardly in praise of education.

A few days later, when Father had his voice again, Lucy overheard Mother say to him, "About Amory's two speeches the other night— do you think he might grow up to be a writer? He certainly has a talent with words, and he knows how to influence people too."

"Influence people!" Father's voice was back to normal. "I should say he can! Do you realize that his Boone story about schooling has influenced the whole township away from building the new school we need? One boy, and he's set us back five or even ten years. Influence! Huh! He's changed the minds of half our taxpayers, and now I've got to try to change them back again."

New Views

THE WEEK after graduation was the Baumgarten
wedding at the Mt. Carmel Catholic church. Mother
and Lucy went with Mrs. Bortz in Bill Bortz's Ford,
first stopping at the Baumgarten farm for Mother to
leave the cut glass celery dish wedding present. Mrs.
Bortz had made enough cookies to feed an army, plus
a dishpanful of potato salad for the dinner.

As they drove in through the farmyard gate, Mr.
Baumgarten was driving the family to the church.
Willie wasn't with them, but Lucy presumed he was
with the groom, since Willie was to be best man.
Lucy found this impressive, though Amory had hooted
at the idea, saying, "Willie's won prizes for his hogs,
but you wait—he'll muddle things somehow." The
auto was full of Baumgartens.

Mary Baumgarten must be in her white wedding dress, but in spite of the heat that day, she was totally wrapped in coats. Mattie, in her bright pink bridesmaid dress, waved and called and was still calling as they drove out of earshot. Mrs. Baumgarten was in the auto too, but she was holding her handkerchief to her eyes, so Lucy knew she must be crying again. Mrs. Baumgarten was a round-faced woman who had so many tears that she shed them on all occasions, exciting or happy or sometimes sad.

Since Mt. Carmel was not on a railroad, it wasn't really a village—more like a crossroads with the big Catholic church the most important building. Lucy stayed out on the church steps for a few minutes with Mrs. Bortz, while Mother went in and began playing the organ. Though Lucy liked listening to grown-up talk, much of this was in German, and what she could understand was not about the wedding but about the long dry spell. The women mourned their gardens, where even the weeds dried up; and the men, in their own group nearby, talked only of drouth and chances of rain and how much crop was already lost.

Always before, Lucy had thought of the farmers' troubles as bad luck for them and bad for Father's business. But now, with Father having a farm and hoping for a big wheat crop that might send her away to school, she listened in a new way. A crop failure would be the end of her secret prophecy.

Once they had gone in, Mrs. Bortz allowed Lucy to sit next to the aisle so she could see everything, from the altar boys and the priest to the bride and groom and Mattie and Willie, the best man. Afterwards it was Willie she couldn't forget. She hadn't seen him much in school this spring because he worked more and more on the farm, and when he did come into town he was in his plaid cotton shirt and overalls.

At the wedding, Willie stood taller than Joe Scheldt, the groom. In fact, he not only stood taller, but he had on a navy blue serge suit with long trousers, his blond hair had been cut by a real barber, and he walked as though he knew what he was doing. When the long mass was over and the wedding party came down the aisle, he saw Lucy and gave her the same crooked smile he'd given her the year before when her tutoring helped him win the improvement prize. But the crooked smile now wasn't shy. It was a wise kind of grin. Willie was on the way to becoming a young man.

All the drive home Lucy pondered, and when the girls came over that afternoon to hear about the wedding, Lucy told them every detail, saving Willie for the climax. "You won't believe it, but Willie's not a kid any more. He's more grown-up than the Boy Scouts, and he's way ahead of us."

Guinevere at once said, "In-cred-ible!" And they all agreed.

"How could he change so much?" Gwin giggled.

"I know what it is," Gwen said. "He's changed because it's a turnabout year, isn't it?"

The drought grew worse each day. Lucy and Amory carried pails of water to keep the garden from drying to a desert, but after the watering, the lettuce and carrots and peas and beans by nightfall looked as dry as before. The bare ground had cracks, and any grassy ground was a brittle tan. Father ceased going out to check on his farm, though by the strange pattern of showers, his farm and the farms near it were harmed but not dried out. "We'll certainly get a crop," he said one night at supper. "Just don't expect the bumper crop we hoped for."

"Enough for going to school in the city?" Lucy asked.

"Perhaps. But I've heard now that I can tutor you here at home for one year so if—"

"I don't want that. I want to go . . ." Lucy saw by Mother's face that this was not the time to argue with Father.

He began to talk with Mother about his oldest sister, Lucy's Aunt Emma, who was visiting in Langdon for a couple of days and then returning to her village in the woods of northern Minnesota. "I don't blame you for not wanting to gallivant all over, Caroline, when George is beginning to grow stronger. But I'd like the children to know her. They barely remember her."

"I don't remember her at all," Lucy said. "She's like a person in a story that you've told me."

"Well, to make her real, I'm taking you and Amory on the Fourth of July to the Langdon cousins' picnic at Walhalla. Your Aunt Emma will be there."

"Walhalla!" Lucy exclaimed.

"Yah, it's where you'll get scalped!" Amory tried to pull his hair into a scalp lock, but his red stiff hair was only an inch long.

"Now what shall I bake for you to take?" said Mother, ignoring the scalping threat.

The Fourth of July was another scorcher and as dry as the preceding fortnight. Lucy bounced alone in the back seat of the Regal, and perhaps it was her imagination, but she thought the front seat escaped all the wind and dust while she sat in the whirl of gritty, blowing dirt.

The Walhalla public picnic park already had crowds of people with their tables spread and their plates of chicken and sandwiches and cakes and pies and pitchers of lemonade covering every inch of table space. Father parked the Regal, and carrying the salad and cake and pie that Mother had sent, they set out to find the other Johnstons. Each year all the families in that Langdon block came here for the Fourth, so Lucy looked for what she'd heard was the "biggest spread of the most to eat in the whole park."

That's how they found it—by the masses of food and her own relatives. Not only were Ed and Len there, but Cousin Gen was home from college and Aunt Emma, of course, was with Aunt Effie and Uncle Charlie. Lucy said hello and noticed that Aunt Emma was no bigger than she was, except that she wore her gray hair coiled on the top of her head and so gained a couple of inches in height.

Aunt Effie, who was alert to Amory's finger, scooping fudge frosting from the edge of the biggest chocolate cake, ordered the children to disappear until they were called.

"We'll be back!" yelled Ed as he and Len and Amory and Lucy ran off. "You kids haven't seen the massacre monument, have you? Let's go there—it's up on that hill."

"Awful far, isn't it?" Lucy panted, trying to keep up.

"Not if we run—gives us an appetite," Amory said, charging up the hill.

Up and up they ran, along a wooded path until they came to a small fenced graveyard, which overlooked the whole broad valley. There inside a low fence stood the granite memorial to the massacred missionaries. Lucy had seen pictures of it, but this was different.

"Under that stone," she said to herself, "are the bodies—no, the bones—well, maybe the dust of the people the Indians killed." And she wished she had another chance to write her opinions of scalping.

The boys stood quietly beside her only a minute. Then Amory suggested, "Say, how about acting out the massacre before we go down to eat? Who'll be a missionary? You, Len?"

"Never!" said Len.

No one volunteered, and Lucy, seeing the three boys had short summer haircuts, could imagine what they were thinking. She turned to run down the hill, and with her head start she stayed ahead, but barely. Behind her the three boys came yelling, "Scalp her! Scalp her!" until they arrived at the picnic table. Lucy had no saintly feelings about those three boys as she came red-faced and panting up to Father. When he remarked, "It's a very hot day to run so hard, but I'm glad you saw your monument," she caught her breath enough to say, "It's not my monument, and I've changed my mind about scalping."

Father made room for her between him and Aunt Emma, and as she squeezed in, she saw in front of her and up and down the table more platters of ham and chicken and sliced roast beef, more salads and pies and cakes than she'd ever seen before, even at a church supper. "All of you have three kinds of cake, children," Aunt Effie said at dessert time. "You have to celebrate the Fourth properly." Lucy chose the tall angel food with pink swirls of frosting, the orange cake topped with orange marshmallows, and the chocolate with dribbles of fudge all down the side. After that, she decided, she wouldn't have to eat again for a week.

Meantime she was listening to Aunt Emma's stories

of how she ran her little newspaper, *The Reporter*, in the village of Roosevelt, Minnesota.

"I've got to be back there tomorrow to get out the next issue and scare up trade for the press—handbills, that kind of thing," she told Father. "I barely make a living, but I do make one, and that's more than most women can say."

Lucy knew this was what Father admired, so she wasn't surprised when he called down the table to Aunt Effie and asked if there was room for Lucy to drive with her and Cousin Gen when they took Aunt Emma home.

"Of course, of course, always room for somebody Lucy's size. We're leaving late this afternoon so we won't have to rush tomorrow."

Another trip, Lucy thought, with delight. The fact that she hadn't a stitch of extra clothes, or even a nightgown didn't faze her. When Father spoke to her before she climbed into the back seat, she understood why he was arranging it. "I want you to see the northern Minnesota forests, and I want you to see another kind of village, Lucy. But mostly I want you to see how a woman gets out a newspaper and makes her own way, even though in her Boston finishing school she was taught to sit and do nothing. Keep your eyes open. Someday you might want to run a newspaper yourself."

Aunt Effie and Gen got into the front seat. Uncle Charlie cranked, and the auto started at once, as the Regal never did. Lucy, packed in the back with Aunt Emma and her suitcases, sat very quiet, watching the totally new road open before her and listening to Aunt Emma's yarns.

They stayed overnight at a hotel in Drayton, and in the morning they rumbled across the long bridge over the Red River of the North. Everyone else called it the Red River; Lucy always thought of it by its full name. "North" suggested the tundra, the Arctic, Eskimos and reindeer.

Around Roseau later in the day, the green woods changed to miles and miles of grotesque black skeletons of trees. "Terrible fire! Forests, villages, farms burned to ashes. People lost everything but the clothes on their backs," Aunt Emma related. Lucy shuddered and for once was glad Wales was a prairie town.

When they came to Lake of the Woods, Lucy stared and stared. It was the most water she'd ever seen in her life. Then Aunt Effie said, "Lucy, did you know that your Uncle Charlie and I were nearly drowned here? A gasoline launch—struck a rock and there we clung, far from shore. Only person for twenty miles was a fisherman. We were saved by him and our prayers."

"Everybody but me has life-and-death experiences," Lucy said to herself. "How can a girl have such a boring life when her relatives have such excitement?"

The village of Roosevelt, however, was no bigger than Wales, and Aunt Emma's square, green-shingled house was about the size of Lucy's home, though it had young birches around it and a strange heap of sawdust and rusting machinery in the front yard. "They sawed the lumber for the house right here," Aunt Emma explained. "I call it my house in the forest, even though the forest is gone. Come in and see my parlor with the tiled fireplace."

Fireplaces impressed Lucy as being far grander than stoves, and this one had shiny green tiles around it.

"Beautifully kept," said Gen. "It looks brand new."

"Built wrong—never been able to use it," Aunt Emma admitted, but she still stood admiring it.

Much of Aunt Emma's house, and her business too, sounded much better when she talked about it then when it was seen first hand. The well water pump was in the kitchen instead of outdoors, but it often didn't pump. One room upstairs had never been plastered, and Lucy saw chinks of light between the boards. Though they'd been hanging for three years, the curtains weren't hemmed, so the next day Aunt Effie and Gen hemmed curtains, while Lucy went with Aunt Emma to her office.

The office was a one-room shop, with most of the space taken by a printing press and a huge rolltop desk. The whole place was a clutter of paper— white paper, stiff green, orange, pink pasteboard, rolls of newspaper without print. On a big table dirty type was tossed in compartmented boxes. And the desk overflowed with envelopes and printed handbills and newspaper clippings and more paper.

Aunt Emma sat down in her swivel chair, shuffled through some mail, and picked up a long page with purple writing. "There's precious little news—I've a reporter in every village, but mostly it's Ladies' Aid meetings, a new baby, or a fire in a chimney. I'll have to stretch it this time."

But before she began stretching her news, Aunt Emma set Lucy to work rolling out sale bills on the little handpress. Lucy worked hard at it, but before the hundredth bill, she knew she had no more knack for presses than she had for knitting. And as for stretching news for a local paper, she was sure Aunt Emma's fantasies were far better than her own.

The drive back to Langdon the next day was simple and fast. When Father came to get her, Mother came along to show George to the relatives. Lucy grabbed him from Mother and rocked him to and fro in her arms. "I missed him, Mother, I truly did."

On the way home, Father asked, "Want to live in a village in the forest, Lucy, and run a newspaper?"

"It's not for me," she replied. "Aunt Emma must be used to forest fires. I'd be scared all the time. And she can get out a whole paper about Ladies' Aid and new babies, and I think she makes her money on handbills that I can't print. But the worst part she says is having to dun people to get what they owe her. I'd hate that. How does she stand it, Father?"

"Well, she may like it because it's such a turnabout from her early life in the East. And then, she's like me— she really enjoys village life, even in a house with cracks between the boards. I'm glad you went, anyway. In three days you saw a lot that was different from Wales and new to you."

"New and different, all right, but it's not what I want," Lucy said. "I want the city or at least a big town and not a village."

Two Tents
in One Camp

THE LAST PART of the drive home was a race against a storm.

"We've had so much dry hot weather lately that I suspect those clouds in the west mean a cloudburst, could even be hail," Father said as he stepped on the accelerator.

"Oh dear, and my peonies at their best," Mother said sadly. "But don't race so, Harry. Thirty miles an hour is far too fast, and why don't we stop and put on the side curtains now before the rain begins?"

Father didn't answer, so Mother wrapped one more blanket around George. Then with her free hand she pushed her hatpins more firmly into her hat. Lucy jounced in the back seat, like popcorn in a popper. The whole sky was now threatening, the masses of dark clouds growing higher and higher. A distant rumble of thunder followed a jagged fork of orange lightning. Father drove faster, Lucy bounced harder, and Mother sat stiffly clutching the baby.

As the first big drops began to fall, they drove up to the big gate, Lucy jumped out, swung it open in record time, and then ran to take the baby from Mother and carry him to the dry porch, while Mother eased herself out of the front seat. Then Father drove the Regal to the barn. He came in the house dripping as though he'd been out in the rain for hours instead of three minutes. "Regular soaker!" Father rubbed his hands delightedly. "Just what the wheat needs, though I fear it could be hail somewhere near us."

He was right. By ten o'clock that night, after the rain had settled to a steady drumming, Father had three phone calls about crops laid flat by hail—Mrs. Towne's oats she said were pounded to oatmeal, Max Schmidt called to thank Father for making him take out hail insurance, and Mr. Hoffer phoned that he hadn't an acre worth harvesting now, but the insurance would buy next year's seed. Finally Father called the Helgesons on his own farm, and the came back grinning.

"Like all hailstorms—freakish! We didn't lose an acre of crop, and this rain will do worlds of good."

After that storm, drought was not a problem, but the weather became hot and humid. "Strange for North Dakota," Father said. "Our heat is always dry heat. Even when it's a hundred degrees, you never feel hot in Dakota."

"I do," Mother contradicted him. "I don't know where you get some of your opinions, Harry—perhaps because you don't cook three meals a day over a coal range."

"Maybe," said Father, "but this damp hot weather is the first I've known in a dozen years here. It can't last long." Yet the humid, overcast, hot days continued until everyone was bad-tempered and the farmers worried that their crops would never ripen without sun. When finally the sun did come out, the air cleared, and everyone cheered up.

"Lucy, your Mother's busy and I want company. Come on, let's see your wheat crop," Father invited. "If it's as good as it should be, I can pay Amory's tuition and send you to the city for a year, too."

Lucy snatched up her bright blue sweater and ran out the door, calling to Mother, "When I get back, I'll shell the peas we picked."

Father had to stop first at the Grangers' to sell insurance on their barn. Mrs. Granger came out to the auto to talk to Lucy while Father did measurements. "You knew our Ted had his number drawn to go into the army? Five from around Wales have to go in the draft, and most of them young like Ted—he's twenty-one, that's young, isn't it?"

Lucy nodded. "And he'll never be the same, going off to army camp and then across the ocean and fighting in those trenches and maybe going to Paris." Mrs. Granger looked sad about all of it, but perhaps saddest about Paris. The Grangers were very strict Methodists, no dancing and no cards. "Mr. Owen came out and talked with us. My, what a comfort that man is. A real help in our troubles." Lucy knew about the drawing of draft numbers and about who had to go, but she was surprised about Mr. Owen's being a comfort. She'd never thought of him that way.

Later when Father had driven along the section road

that bordered his farm, he stopped the auto beside the acres of wheat. "Look! a wheat gold mine, Lucy. I'll pick you some, just to show you how lucky you are. That spell of the northern lights," he joked, "must be foolproof. Both the drought and the hail passed this by." He got out and picked several heads of the wheat, rubbing them together in his hand as Lucy had often seen him do to predict a good or a bad crop. But this time he put them close to his face, dumped the handful to the ground, walked into the field a few feet, picked a second handful, rubbed the heads and again threw them down.

He repeated this several times, always going a little farther into the sunny field of grain. The sun shone down warmly, but the slight breeze kept the air comfortable, and it waved the tall wheat like waves in a big lake.

Father came back to the auto, carrying an armful of wheat—roots, stalks, and heads. She reached out her hands for it. "Can I have it all?" she asked.

"You can have the whole blamed crop. Nobody else will pay a penny for it. The humid spell did it—all blighted. What I've got is a crop of rust."

Lucy knew what rust was, and she'd heard of great losses elsewhere a couple of summers ago from overcast humid weather, so she asked nothing. She understood. The wheat looked handsome on the outside. Inside not a kernel had formed. The crop wasn't worth threshing—not worth a cent.

They drove home in silence. Mother came to the back door. "Supper's not ready yet. You're home very early." Then she saw Father's face. "What's happened, Harry?"

"Our whole crop's gone—every single head on every stalk rusted to nothing, nothing at all." He went into the living room.

"Lucy, take George out in his carriage and walk over to Fischers'. Amory was invited to have supper there, and now I think it's a good idea. Then bring George home, give him his bottle and put him to bed. I'm going out to the farm with your father. It could be only the few stalks he picked—could be, but I'm afraid . . ."

The folks were gone when Lucy brought the baby back, and after he was in bed, she ate the supper Mother had left for her. She was reading *A Tale of Two Cities* when Amory came home.

When he asked, "How come that you're alone?" she told him. And she added, "You better get that scholarship or I'm stuck here."

After a couple of clear days, the weather turned hot and humid again. Now everyone complained louder than ever, for the wheat crop and the farmers' hopes were ruined and yet the unnatural damp heat continued, almost tropical. Then unexpectedly Lucy had a little luck from the sultry dog days. She had been weeding the garden and came into the kitchen, perspiring and wretched. Mother looked at her quickly and then looked a second time. "Well I never!" she said. "Do you know, Lucy, that in this dampness the hair around your face is curling?"

"Curling?" Lucy ran to the small mirror that hung by the kitchen window, and there she surveyed the miracle. Her red hair that had always been straight as a string was curling, the short hairs next to her cheeks actually in small ringlets. "Could it happen all at once?" she asked Mother.

"More likely we've had our minds on so much else

that we weren't seeing. I do believe if you lived by the sea, you'd have wavy hair from the moist air."

"Okay! When I grow up, I'll live near the sea," Lucy said very definitely, before she ran upstairs to look in a larger mirror. She could hardly wait to show the Owens.

This year the Hannah congregation had grown while the Wales one had shrunk. Protestants had moved away, and Catholics had moved in. So the Owens spent much of their time in Hannah, living in the large furnished parsonage the church there had bought. Always when they came home to Wales, the girls immediately phoned Lucy. On the first day of August they phoned, Gwen and Gwin both talked at once, and all Lucy could understand were the words, "We're moving! We're moving!" and "We'll be right over."

Soon Lucy saw them coming and ran to the back gate, calling, "Where you moving to? When? Is it in Canada?"

"Ottawa, the capital city of Canada. So my prophecy came true," Guinevere said smugly. "In-cred-ible, isn't it?"

"It's not really Ottawa, but a village near it. The Bishop there wrote that they need ministers in Canada now because so many are in the army as chaplains. Papa couldn't get a church there last year and the churches here needed someone," Gwen explained. "In another year, I'll go to high school in Ottawa, just the way you'll go to a city high school, Lucy, when your father's crop comes in."

Lucy felt too disappointed to tell her bad news. This once she welcomed Edward's arrival. "I'm going to get me a velocipede and ride all over the city," Edward shouted. Then he spread his arms and clenched his hands as though he held handle bars and raced in big circles into the garden.

"Ed-ward!" Lucy yelled. "You're trampling Father's cucumbers and squash. Come back here on the walk, or he'll give you what-for." Even a mention of Father brought Edward into line.

Mother was in the kitchen. The news was told a second time, and Gwin added, "Did you know that after this, the Wales minister isn't going to be?"

"Isn't going to be? What on earth do you mean?"

"That was in the bishop's letter, too," Gwin told them. "After the Methodist conference in the fall the Methodist minister will live in Hannah and come to Wales only now and then. So it's good you're going away to school, Lucy. Nobody'll be here."

Mother glanced at Lucy. She'd have to tell them about the blighted crop. "Unless Amory gets a scholarship, I can't go away. All the wheat crops around Wales are blighted, and Father's—well, his is a total loss. Most likely I'll just stay in Wales for a year, and he'll tutor me."

"Oh, I wish I could stay here with you," Gwen said and gave Lucy a hug.

Gwin glared out the window at Amory, coming along the back path. "There's that Amory. He's got what he wants—he'll go away to school and wear that lovely uniform and ride home for Christmas vacation on a Pullman. Lucy, where's your luck?"

"My hair's turning curly, and that's luck," Lucy said. But only Gwen was impressed. The other two girls had long curls already.

Nothing had been said for a long time about the camping trip Father had promised for both clubs before the Owens left. Now time was getting short, since the

Owens would leave early in September. So the next day Lucy asked Father, "Can you still take us camping on the Pembina this month if we're so poor?"

"We're not poor. What a thing to say! We just can't have everything. Of course I'll take you camping— cheapest holiday there is, and the best one, too."

"Stan's working at Dunns' farm with his father, and Jerry's getting paid for jobs around his father's farm machinery store. So I'll be the only boy with that bunch of girls," Amory complained.

"No, you won't be. Mr. Owen asked me to take Edward, and I couldn't refuse him. But I need you as a second man around the camp. And you've not yet tried your birthday rod and reel. I hear it's still good fishing in the river."

A fortnight before this, Amory had turned thirteen, and the only present he'd asked for was an expensive rod and reel. Since Lucy thought fishing was a bore, she was glad her birthday present would be something better. But Mother thought the fishing tackle a wise choice. "It's not like a gun. You can't possibly hurt anybody with a rod and reel," she had said.

Father and Amory made long lists of fishing tackle to take, and Mother and Lucy planned food and warm clothes and bedding.

"If you can't catch any fish, you can always fix bean-hole beans," Mother said.

"We'll catch whole strings of fish, and I'll bet I catch the biggest fish that ever saw the Pembina River," Amory bragged.

"I can make pancakes, if they don't get fish," Lucy put in. "And you give us enough all-cooked food for the first meals and—"

"And how about butterscotch pies? That's a good

sweet dessert we'd all like," Armory added.

"With seven of us packed in the Regal, someone would certainly sit on pies." Father then went on, "But how about marshmallows to roast for dessert? And Caroline, now that you hear about all this food and fishing and tent life, don't you want to put your little papoose on your back and come along too?"

"No, thank you. I'm happy to have him for an excuse to stay home. But how will you pack everything in?" She shook her head. "And when I think of the flat tires you're going to have . . ."

"I'm borrowing Joe Klein's trailer for most of the load, though that may pull the rear end out of the Regal," he teased.

"Don't joke, Harry. Camping is a new experience for the Owens, and we want it to go well. Lucy, when you tell them about all this, be sure to explain it's a roughing-it, rugged trip and not a tea party."

With Mrs. Owen, Edward was the only worry. "I'm not sure what he should wear, Lucy. If you met anyone in Canada, I'd like him to look nice, and then there's the river. Does your father watch all of you every minute?"

Lucy hoped for a time that Mrs. Owen's fears would be enough to keep Edward home, but no such luck. When the trailer with two tents and blankets and kettles and clothes and ropes and tackle and food was finally packed, and the Regal had four girls piled in the back seat, there was Edward up front between Father and Amory. The Owens came over to give last minute instructions about the care of Edward, and as the loaded trailer and auto full of children pulled out to the road, Mother waved serenely but Mr. and Mrs. Owen looked as though they were waving good-bye forever.

At the tiny village of Snowflake, Manitoba, they stopped at the Canadian customs office to report to the man in charge. Ever since the war, Canada had been very strict about who crossed the border, and why, and for how long. Amory stayed in the auto, but all the rest of them trooped in with Father. The officer listed everybody. "Four Canadians and three Yankees on a camp trip? Fine! But be sure to check out when you leave. There's an alert along this part of the border right now. We're looking for someone crossing to the States." He laughed and said, "Not that we'd suspect a man with six kids was a lawbreaker. You must really like kids, or is it the camping?"

"Both," Father answered, and they were on their way again.

The small plateau partway up the riverbank was thickly wooded on three sides, and there was no road in to it. But everyone was so glad to get out of the crowded auto that lugging the stuff through the woods to the campsite was fun. The two tents were up in record time, the girls tying the ropes quite as well as Father or Amory. Everyone foraged for firewood, Father fixed a hanging kettle of water over the campfire, the girls spread out the food Mother had prepared, and as they ate, everything was perfect.

When Father later proposed fishing for Amory and him, Edward refused to stay with the girls. But Father went on checking his rod and reel, and Amory practised casting down by the river. Finally Edward tried tears. "I'll cry, Mr. Johnston."

"Cry very softly then. We don't want anything to scare the fish," Father replied, picking up his tackle and going down to join Amory at the river. From there he called back, "We may bring back fish for supper. We're going upriver a way."

For the afternoon, the girls took turns keeping Edward from pulling up tent stakes, getting too close to the fire, or eating all the marshmallows in great gulps. Later they went wading in a shallow pool, since the river was too low in August for real swimming. By suppertime, Amory and Father came back without a single fish, but they were so full of fishing plans for the next day that they didn't seem to mind. And Mother had sent along so much ready-to-eat food that they cooked only the kettleful of beans over the fire that night to bury later in a hole under the ashes for an all-night baking.

Father was the expert on beanhole beans, and he carefully measured beans and salt pork and brown sugar and water. While they hunted for large flat stones to heat and bury with the closed kettle and hot coals, Edward was alone for five minutes. When they returned carrying stones, he was leaning over the fire. "Edward!" Gwen screamed. "Don't lean so close to that boiling kettle of beans."

"I got to, or else I won't find it," Edward said crossly.

"Won't find what?" Lucy asked.

"My gum," he answered, and if Gwen hadn't caught him by the seat of the pants, he'd have toppled into the fire.

"Your gum's missing? Where did you lose it?" Father came up the riverbank.

"It fell into your beans, Mr. Johnston. And it was a great big hunk, too."

"Well of all the—of all the . . ." Father never finished

the sentence, probably not a sentence to say to a minister's boy.

Lucy picked up a long spoon and began stirring and stirring, but no gum came to the surface. Amory was furious. "Has that kid spit his gum in our beans? I won't eat a single bean until it's fished out. It's not sanitary!"

Father got a shovel, pushed aside the hot coals, dug the hole, and put in the kettle with coals and stones and hot dirt over it. Edward stood scowling.

Only
in Books

FATHER BUILT UP the fire again, and the gum was forgotten as everyone sharpened sticks for roasting the marshmallows. Surrounded by woods, the camp was soon dark except for the blazing fire. Once the marshmallows were gone, they sang a few songs, but first Edward and then Guinevere began to lean sleepily on the older sisters, so Father suggested bed. And no one objected, especially to going to bed in a tent.

The next morning's breakfast was beanhole beans. Father shoveled aside the embers of the fire and dug down for the pot of beans. The only trouble was that his shovel knocked off the cover and dirt took its place, so that when he lifted out the kettle, with all six of the children watching their breakfast rise from the ground, they saw baked sand instead of baked beans.

"A little dirt in the diet is good for you," Father stated, and he scooped and skimmed to get down to the beans. "There! Just smell that aroma." He began ladling out the beans to each tin plate. "Nothing like camp food, is there, children?"

Lucy was used to Father's beans, and this wasn't the first time he'd added dirt to the recipe, but Guinevere ate her helping bean by bean, and Edward complained, "I keep looking for my gum, but somebody else has got it."

"It's all cooked in now, Edward," Gwen explained. "But maybe that's what makes these beans so good. I never ate any like this before. Real taste of the camp."

"Dirt, gum, and ants," Amory said sourly, but he ate three helpings and half a bottle of catsup. "Now for some fishing. Today's the day I catch my whopper." Since Father was as devoted to fishing as Amory, they both went off very soon. The girls went down to the river, but not for fishing.

Edward trailed a stick in the water with a hook and string, Guinevere collected colored pebbles, and all of them waded for a while along the sandy side of the river. "Don't you wish our mothers were here?" Gwen asked. "It's so peaceful. And look at that clump of loosestrife upstream, and highbush cranberries—bunches of berries. Should we pick some?" But it was a lazy morning and no one picked anything, only talked and waded.

Suddenly, from a little way up the river came a scream. "Luuucy! Luuucy! I need you!" Definitely it was Amory calling her, but never in his life had Amory yelled that he needed her, so for a moment Lucy stood unmoving, until the scream came again. "Come quick!"

Lucy pulled her skirts higher and splashed up the

stream, slipping now and then on the wet stones, but never falling. Behind her splashed the Owens, with Edward wailing, "Wait for me!" Around a bend in the river stood Amory with Father sitting on the shore beside him. "Look!" screamed Gwin. And Lucy did look.

Caught in Father's ear was a large barbed fishhook, baited with a piece of worm. The line on the hook came from the rod that Amory still held. Father was leaning against a big rock, probably the only boulder for fifty miles around. He looked very groggy and unsure of himself.

"What's going on?" piped Guinevere in her squeaky voice.

"Isn't that a fishhook in your ear, Mr. Johnston?" Edward asked. "Isn't that a mistake?"

At these Owen comments, Lucy saw Father coming back to life very fast, but he still leaned limply on the boulder. When Lucy was beside him, she saw a small trickle of blood down the back of his head. Amory explained. "I was casting with my new reel and I swung too far. He must have seen it coming, and when he stepped back he slipped, and wham—he hit his head. Now, Lucy, you get out the fishhook."

"You can't get that out without a doctor, Amory. It's really hooked—and I don't think that worm's very sanitary, either." Lucy began to feel as ill as Father looked.

Amory still planned first aid at camp. "I'd use my jackknife, and it's a lot sharper than the carving knife, but the trouble is—well, I always cut bait with it."

Father lifted his head, and then let it slowly drop back. Lucy took it as a very bad sign that he said not a word. Ordinarily he'd blow up at Amory.

"If you use camp knives, he'll get blood poisoning," Gwen warned.

"Will he die?" asked Edward in a mournful voice.

"Killed by his own son!" Guinevere added. "That's the worst of it."

Father lifted his head again, and this time he sat up. He reached back, touched his head, and brought his hand around in front again. "I can't be bleeding much, so it's this blamed hook we've got to get out." Then he rallied more. "I'm not going to die and a fishhook never killed anybody, but I must look like a fool. Lucy, hold the hook steady. Amory, cut that good new line of yours."

When that was done, Father stood up, the hook still dangling from the lobe of his ear. "I'll not trust camp surgery with you amateurs. I've got to drive to the nearest doctor—Crystal City. Bring the stuff up with you, children." Glad of something they could do, everybody carried rods and tackle boxes up to the camp, while Father, leaning on Amory, trailed behind them.

By the time Lucy had poured half a bottle of peroxide on the back of Father's head, he was revived enough to plan the rest of the day. "Gwen, make Amory a couple of big peanut butter sandwiches. He's got to come with me, in case I get a flat or have to send him for help, but he'll be no good if he's hungry."

"Make it four sandwiches," Amory ordered, "and the rest of that chocolate cake."

Father went on. "Get my other jacket out of the tent, Lucy. And all of you listen to me. I hope to be back before supper, but if I'm not, you know how to make pancakes." Then Father revived enough to joke. "Don't spit in the pancake batter, Edward; and since you're the only man here, you take good care of the girls."

Amory picked up his lunch, and Father and he set off through the woods toward the parked auto. Edward followed them a few steps, swaggering with his new importance. The last thing Lucy saw was the hook swaying to and fro beside Father's cheek.

"It looks like a big tin earring, doesn't it?" giggled Gwin. Then she saw Lucy's worried expression and she said no more. They ate a quiet lunch, finishing the kettle of beanhole beans. The rest of the day they were by the river again, repeating everything they'd done in the morning. But now nothing was very much fun, and Edward, as the "only man," insisted upon bossing them.

Finally Lucy left the Owens and climbed to the camp to check the fire and mix the pancakes. "I'll call you when I'm ready for you to help," Lucy told them. But once she was up at the camp, she was so glad to get away from Edward that she fixed the fire and made the pancakes and had just put a trial one in the frying pan when she went to the river side of the plateau to call them.

Before she could open her mouth, however, two men came out of the woods very near her. At first she thought she'd never seen them before. They weren't dressed for camping or fishing, but their city suits looked as though they'd been roughing it for days—muddy and wrinkled and torn in places. The taller man went directly to the campfire. He picked up the pancake turner and flipped her trial pancake, stirred up the bowl of batter, and dropped in two more pancakes before Lucy knew what he was doing.

"Those are my pancakes," she told him, as she went toward the fire. "I made them and you can't . . ." She didn't finish, for she had come close enough to take the turner away from him, and as she reached for it, she saw his right hand. There was the crushed forefinger. She quickly look up at the man's face, and recognized Toby Mitchell.

He scowled at her as though he were puzzled. "Seen you before, haven't I? I remember that hair. Where did I see you, kid?"

"At the Wales school," she answered. "In Miss Hoffer's room."

"Yes. So you know who I am." He still held the turner and flipped the other two pancakes before he lifted out the sample one. Then without butter or syrup, he wolfed that pancake in four bites, tossing the hot cake from one hand to the other as he ate. "I'll take the other two for my friend, and we'll be on our way," he said, flipping the two on a tin plate nearby and carrying it to the short blond man, who had never left the shade of the woods.

Lucy stood stupidly dumb while Toby dropped the plate to the ground after his friend had snatched the pancakes. This man was also vaguely familiar, but Lucy was so thunderstruck by the whole event that she watched the two men disappear in the deep woods without really knowing what she was seeing.

Once they were out of sight, she ran down the bank, yelling, "Supper's ready!"

The Owens came scrambling to the camp, Edward screaming, "I'm as hungry as—as AMORY!" To gather her wits, Lucy concentrated on pancakes, spooning out the batter to the pan, turning the cakes expertly, and passing them out to each shiny tin plate, until everyone had an equal share. The syrup was poured on until the can was nearly gone, and finally every plate was empty.

Only then did Lucy startle them with her news. "While I was here alone, two men came. One was Toby Mitchell and he looked as though he'd been living in the woods, but not camping. And he was so hungry— he ate my sample pancake right from the fire."

"Toby Mitchell? Without his white silk shirt?" Gwen asked. "Are you sure, Lucy? It's not dark, but it's kind of twilight."

"I'm sure, because he's got a crushed finger just like mine. And do you know what I think?" Lucy paused to get the full effect. "I think—no, I'm sure he was the detective's driver on New Year's Day. The one that my father said was either a dummy or a crook too bright for the detective."

"The spy again?" Gwin was ready to start off through the woods after the men.

"The other man with him—who was he?" asked Gwen. "Did you ever see him before?"

"I've got a feeling that—yes, I've seen him, but I don't know where."

"Think! Think hard! Do your duty by Canada and your country, Lucy," Guinevere commanded.

But Lucy's thinking was interrupted by a WAHOO! from Amory, followed by Father's whistle of Bob- WHITE that was their family call. Amory ran from the woods, Father came behind with his ear in a crisscross of gauze and tape, and beside Father walked a Canadian policeman, a Mounty in his uniform. He took off his wide hat as he came forward and Father introduced him.

"This is Sergeant Gordon. We met him here when we parked the auto. He's looking for some men he wants. Answer his questions."

"Have any strangers been here this afternoon?" he asked sternly.

"Yes, and one was Toby Mitchell and the other was—" Lucy stopped because suddenly she remembered where she'd seen the short blond man. "The other one was the butcher's cousin. That's who it was." Before she could go on, Amory took over.

"Our butcher's name is Berman, and Toby Mitchell spent only a little while in Wales, mostly at the blind pig that the Morgans run, and I'm sorry I wasn't here today to catch those men for you, but you see I caught my father by the ear so we were away." As an after-thought, he added, "I had a worm for bait."

The Mounty had stood staring at Amory, but at this last bit of information, he burst out laughing and so did Father. "I'll remember to use a worm next time I'm sent out to get my man," Sergeant Gordon said, when he'd finally stopped laughing. "Now boy, let your sister answer a question or two. Toby Mitchell and Hans Berman are two of the men we're looking for, but was there any third man here?"

"No," said Lucy. "Only two men ate the pancakes I made."

"Ate my sister's pancakes? Poor guys, they're dead by now."

The Mounty turned to Father. "The third man is a Mike Morgan of that Morgan family your son connects with the blind pig. Do you know anything about him?"

"The only thing I've heard about him lately," Father replied, "is that he left town New Year's night and hasn't been seen since."

"And what about the butcher's cousin, as you call him?"

This was Gwin's chance to talk. "We girls all saw him once. We think he came from Canada and went back maybe, and in his heavy satchel he had whisky bottles. Anyway we think so, but our papa is a minister and we don't know that much about—"

"Surprising bunch of young ones you've got here," the Sergeant interrupted. "I'd enjoy staying longer, but I've got to go search for these men. In the woods it's already dark and they've got a head start, aiming for the border, of course. Thank you all, and good night." He put on his hat again, waved and left.

The rest of the firewood was piled on. They sat in a circle near the blaze and talked so much and so long that finally Father looked at his watch. "Almost ten o'clock, and we'll have to be up very early to pack for home. To bed, everybody!" And though the girls whispered awhile in their tent about Mounties and spies, even they soon fell asleep.

Breakfast was a fast meal of cold cereal and toast burned over the fire. In no time the tents were down, the camping gear was piled in the trailer, buckets of river water were poured on the campfire ashes, and the Regal with its heaped trailer pulled out to the road. At Snowflake, they stopped again at the border office, and there even Amory got out to learn the news of last night's search.

A different officer was there, but Father asked for news after he explained what had happened at camp. "They got across, probably all three," the officer said. "And once they've crossed to the States, you know, we can't get them back without a lot of evidence for a crime." He shook his head almost sadly. "Pity your kids didn't catch them yesterday, right here in Canada."

"Maybe it's my fault," Father said, smiling. "I've always told them it's only in books that children catch the lawbreakers. So they weren't prepared."

In spite of Mother's fears, the trip both ways was

made without a single flat tire. They were back in Wales by noon. At the parsonage, the Owens got out, and Mrs. Owen came flying out the front gate to embrace Edward. Then she saw Father's bandage and heard the fishhook story. "Good gracious, it might have happened to Edward," she said. And though she thanked Father warmly for taking the children, she continued to hang onto Edward as though he'd just been rescued from death.

As they drove into the yard at home, Mother got up from weeding her asters and hurried to the auto. "I'm so glad you had good weather and did you do what you said you would, Amory? Did you catch the biggest fish that ever saw the Pembina River? And Harry, what on earth happened to your ear?"

"I was the poor fish, Caroline. So yes, he did catch the biggest one that ever saw the Pembina."

That night at supper they were still discussing the Mounty's search for the three wanted men. "It must be for something they were doing in Canada, some illegal way of getting money," Father said. "Toby certainly spent more money on his clothes and at the blind pig than he earned at the pool hall. And from what the girls say, the butcher's cousin was dressed like a city slicker. All that costs money."

"I suppose it's almost too neat that Toby was the detective's driver, and after he went to the blind pig, Mike Morgan skipped town? Was there spying after all?" Lucy spoke hesitantly, since she didn't want Father to blow up again about spy hunting.

"We'll never know," Father answered. "But one thing I did learn this afternoon. Old man Morgan is shutting the blind pig—for good."

"For good, all right!" Mother echoed him. "Is it because he's the only one left here to run it now?"

"Could be, but I suspect it's because there's all that talk about a constitutional amendment making the whole USA like North Dakota, with prohibition the law. Small-time operators like Morgan don't want to get in trouble with federal officers. A county sheriff is different."

"Well, no blind pig in Wales! That's a change none of you prophesied on New Year's Eve, isn't it, Harry? And they're not looking for Danny Morgan? Perhaps Danny wasn't in all this."

To herself, Lucy said, "He's safe—he's saved by falling in love with Lily." But she wouldn't have said it out loud for worlds. Amory would hoot and the folks would preach.

The day after the camping trip was Lucy's twelfth birthday. Mother and Mrs. Owen had prepared a birthday tea, as Mrs. Owen called it, and each of the girls had made a present: Gwen had written a ten-page diary about their year in Wales, and Gwin had drawn a tiny picture for each event, from the first drive in the Regal to Father's hooked ear; Guinevere had collected postcards from eastern Canada for Lucy, and Edward gave her tin foil from two packages of gum. The gum he had chewed, of course.

At supper that night Lucy got her family presents. Mother gave her a fountain pen and Father had bought her a dictionary for her coming year of tutoring at home. Amory gave her one of his war posters, and the Langdon cousins gave her the best present of all, a wristwatch on a black ribbon bracelet with a silver snap. No present had ever made her feel so grown-up. "A woman's watch," she said to herself. "I'm changing. I know I am."

Good-bye!
Good-bye!

BY NOW summer was ending, and Lucy felt everything else was ending also. The Owens were leaving on September fifth, and five days later Amory must go, on the very day the Wales school would open. Later Jerry would go to the Langdon high school, and after the harvest Stan and his folks were moving to the East Coast. Only Lucy was going nowhere, not even to the Wales school.

Father had ordered an algebra book for her and dusted off his old Latin grammar. Amory gave her his favorite ancient history book, and Father Van Mert offered to teach her beginner's French. "It's a wonderful opportunity, Lucy. Why, you may cover two years' work in one," Father said enthusiastically. "It's much better than your being swallowed up in that big city high school."

Since there was no money to pay for her to be "swallowed up," Lucy didn't argue. The folks never talked of their crop disaster nor of their hope of a scholarship for Amory. Mother filled the house with great bunches of asters and marigolds from her garden, planned projects for herself and Lucy after the Owens were gone, and always she played her most cheerful music.

In spite of the bad crop, fall was Father's favorite season as always. He insisted that they go outdoors to admire the brilliant sunsets spread across the entire western sky. When huge V's of Canada geese flew honking over the village on their way south, Father stood in the yard, his head thrown back, calling, "There they go! Nothing like it! The most beautiful sight in the world!" Late one night the northern lights were bright enough for him to wake Lucy to see them from the back kitchen window. "They're not so bright as last year, but I'm sure they still cast their spell on you —Lucky Lucy." He was teasing, so Lucy didn't answer.

What she wanted to say was, "What's so lucky about being left here when everybody goes away?" The secret prophecy bothered her also. She'd promised to show everyone next New Year's Day what she'd written on the slip of paper, and now she'd look so stupid that she was glad the Owens would be far away in Ottawa. She'd never hear what they'd say about her when they opened their letter in January.

With their packing and spending time in Hannah and going to farewell suppers at every Methodist home, the Owens were seldom at the Johnstons' house the last fortnight before they left. It was then that Lucy found the baby as much fun as she had dreamed before he was born. He was out of his long white dresses and into short ones that she enjoyed putting on him. She wheeled him and fed him and rocked him, and he paid her in smiles and in going to her arms as readily as to Mother's. He'd never be a girl, but in everything else he was a total success.

Then came the news that the men whose numbers were drawn in the draft must leave on September fifth, the very day the Owens were going. Wales was agog with two such big events at once. Mr. Fraser, who played the cornet very well, organized a village brass band of seven instruments to play at the station for the send-off of the drafted men. Though only five men were called up from the township, the whole country-side would be there to say good-bye.

Because she thought the crowd would be bad for the baby, Mother said her farewell to the Owens in the morning, and Lucy went over to the parsonage with her. The tiny house was so dismal that she and Gwen went out into the yard. There they both promised never to forget each other, to write each other very, very often, and to see each other when they were grown-up and could go where they liked. They both began to cry, so Lucy ran for home before the younger Owens could make fun of them.

That afternoon when the train from Hannah drew in, the platform was jammed with people. Every store in the village was shut for half an hour, and even Father's bank was closed. Women were crying, children were waving tiny flags and running helter-skelter through the crowd, and men had come from the fields in order to wish the soldiers luck. Lucy knew that men

just called up couldn't yet have uniforms, but five
young men in their Sunday suits were not as exciting
as she wished. The brass band was far better.

Mr. Quimby drove up with all the Owens packed
into his Ford, barely in time. At the same moment that
they went toward the waiting train, Father hurried up
to Lucy. "I can't find Amory, so you'll be the first to
know. Ten minutes ago your grandfather wired.
Amory has his scholarship—full tuition."

To be heard over the brass band, now playing "Pack
Up Your Troubles in Your Old Kit Bag," Lucy

screamed at Father. "Now can I go to the city for high school?"

"Yes," Father yelled back at her. "I've not peeked, but I suspect you might want your secret prophecy—to show the Owens?" He handed her the envelope with LUCY JOHNSTON'S PRIVATE PROPERTY printed on it.

Lucy grabbed it, tearing it open as she ran to the group of people standing around the Owens at the coach steps. She heard Edward saying, "Is the band for me, like for the Prince of Wales?" She caught the sound of Gwin's soprano high over the crowd's chorus of "Smile, Smile, Smile." And then she was beside train. Gwen was already in the vestibule, smiling and waving, just as she had months ago when the Owens arrived.

"Gwen!" Lucy yelled. "Amory got his scholarship. I'll go away to school. And look—my secret prophecy!" She pulled the paper from the envelope, Gwen reached down for it, quickly read it, and then so loud that the other Owens could hear her, she shouted, waving the paper, "Lucy's secret prophecy is coming true. She's going away to a big city school."

Guinevere was climbing the steps so Gwen handed her the paper to hand to Lucy, and for once Lucy agreed with Guinevere's exclamation. "In-cred-ible, Lucy. In-cred-ible!"

The Owens, one by one, went through the vestibule and appeared at windows of the coach, while the five future Wales soldiers climbed to the vestibule of the smoker and stood more or less at attention while the band played "The Star-Spangled Banner." Mr. Fraser had trained the band to shift after one verse to "My Country 'Tis of Thee." Of this Lucy was very glad, for watching the faces of the Owen girls at the coach windows, she knew they were singing, too. And she knew they were singing their own words to the same tune—"God Save the King."

The train pulled out, the crowd moved along Main Street in small knots of people, and Lucy rushed home. There Mother was on the phone, learning the news from Father, and when she hung up, her first words to Lucy were, "We have five days to get you ready. I suppose we can make it."

Lucy grinned. "I suppose we can. And Mother, don't buy me anything new here. I'd rather wait to see what girls wear this fall in the city. But what about a trunk?"

So Father hitched the trailer to the Regal, and they drove to Langdon to buy a small trunk. When it was bought and Father was roping it on the trailer, Mother and Lucy visited with Aunt Effie. She once more invited Lucy to come live with them in another year, if she should find the city wasn't what she liked. Lucy couldn't imagine not wanting the city high school, but as always she liked feeling this Langdon house was her second home and the Langdon cousins were her second family.

The days passed so rapidly that Lucy thought of nothing but her trip and the city and her year ahead. Then the last night at home, Mother and Father went for a drive, and Lucy baby-sat for the last time. She was rocking George to sleep, cradling him in her arms, when suddenly she realized that the next night she'd be on the Empire Builder and for months after that, until Christmas, she wouldn't see George at all, let alone rock him and cuddle him.

Unaccountably, she began to cry. Amory was reading on the floor. He looked up, saw her tears, and asked, "What's wrong?"

"I don't know. I think maybe I'm homesick, while

I'm still at home. Oh, Amory I'm not sure I want to go away to school after all."

He sat up. "Do you think I want to go?" Lucy stared at him. "I never told you, but at that academy I'll have to do everything by bells and shouted orders, and you do a lot of drill, and those guns are heavy, and there's a lot of going to church. It's not my kind of place. And I'll be the smallest kid there, and I'll get pushed around, and those heavy uniforms are hot and tight and you have to keep your shoes shined—not just Sundays, but every day. And. . . . Well, I'm going to hate it. I hate it already." He lay down flat on his stomach again to continue reading.

"But Amory, I thought you wanted to go. You always talk so big about going away to prep school, so I thought—"

"I've got to go, so it wouldn't do any good to gripe. But you're lucky, Lucy. You can come back next year and live at Aunt Effie's if you don't like Central High School."

"Maybe you could live in Langdon or at Grandfather's in the city?" Lucy suggested.

"I think maybe the relatives all somehow got the idea I'm a—perhaps a—"

"A handful?"

"Uh-huh, that's about it." And Amory went on reading, leaving Lucy with a whole new idea to think about.

The following day the train was on time, so school was still in session when Lucy and Mother wheeled the carriage toward the station. The trunks were packed and ready on the platform. Father was to meet them there. Amory was with Stan and Jerry, who both had time off to say good-bye to him.

Until they went out of the yard and along the board

walk, Lucy hadn't thought of all the people who would say good-bye as she and Mother went to the train. Mrs. Schnitzler came out and held up a Red Cross sock she was knitting. "Don't forget the heel—*ein, zwei, drei*," she called. Mrs. Flint came to her gate, saying, "What a pity your family doesn't move to the city, perhaps to St. Paul. Then you wouldn't have to go away—and so young too." Mother only nodded in reply.

Mrs. Kinser rapped on her window and smiled her good-bye. The empty church and the empty parsonage made Lucy lonesome, but after that was the school and she knew that wasn't empty. This year it was crammed with children. Lucy heard a banging on the upstairs window of her old school room, and looking up, she saw a crowd of faces—everyone from Cyril and Harvey to Julie Meizner and Mary Hoffer, who was back this year to teach in the same room. Lucy waved back as hard as she could, and she was still waving as they came to the priest's house.

Father Van Mert was getting in vegetables from his garden, with Magic at his feet. "Good-bye, Lucy, and I'm sorry I won't be teaching you French. I've translated that letter from your French Lucie that came yesterday, and she wants you to know she's learning to knit socks for the soldiers."

Lucy stopped in amazement. "That five-year-old is knitting socks?" Mother went ahead with the carriage.

Mrs. Ludwig came out the back door. "Oh, my, she's a bright little French girl. All little girls in Europe, though, all knit socks and scarves and sweaters and—"

"Caw! Caw! Caw!" Magic drowned her out. Father Van Mert smiled a good-bye, and Lucy ran to catch up. In front of the butcher shop, she paused as Ed the butcher came out with a small brown bag.

"I heard you and your brother were going today. Here's a bag of those cookies with the pink top that you like. Good luck." He went right back in his shop before Lucy could say thank you. She hoped he'd never learned about her thinking him a spy. But that seemed years ago.

At the bank, Father joined them, and in front of Lowensteins' they met the three Boy Scouts, each with a big bag of candy. "I just went in to say good-bye," Amory explained, "and look—a striped candy bag full of more candy than we can eat, or almost more." And the boys ran ahead to the station.

"We don't have long to wait, and that's good," Father said, as they all came to the platform together. "Amory, here's the envelope that has tickets and baggage checks. Put it in your inside jacket pocket and button that flap over it. You're in charge." Amory stood very seriously while Father watched him stow the valuable pieces of paper.

"Lucy, I don't have another prophecy of yours to give you at the last moment, but the mail was sorted only a few minutes ago and there's a card from Minneapolis for you." Father took from his pocket a colored postcard of Minnehaha Falls.

"Named for Hiawatha's wife!" Lucy exclaimed. "And I'll soon see those wonderful falls."

"Don't get your hopes up. That picture must have been taken after a cloudburst. They're only a trickle now, so that poet Longfellow lied to you again, didn't he?" Father teased.

"Who's the card from?" Mother asked.

Lucy turned it over. "From Ben Larson, the boy next door to Grandfather, and he says—why, as soon as he heard I was coming, he sold that girl's bike to

Grandfather to give me for a present, and he's throwing in lessons on how to ride it."

Father laughed. "He sounds like an operator to me, Lucy. Don't you fall for a city slicker while you're away."

Then the train whistled at the north crossing, and Tom Evans came out with the mailbags. Suddenly Lucy felt very unsure about everything. "Oh, Mother, I don't know—I should know what I want to do, but I . . . Won't I ever grow up and know what I want for sure?"

Mother was crying a little, so it was Father who answered. "You're only twelve, but you've grown up a lot this year—a turnabout, I'd call it. You're ready for something new."

The train ground to a stop, the conductor got off, Amory thumped each boy, shook hands with Father, kissed Mother with a loud smack and jumped to the vestibule.

Lucy leaned over the carriage to kiss George, who thought she was going to pick him up so he held out his arms to her. She touched his hands, quickly threw her arms first around Mother and then around Father, and climbed on the train. There in the vestibule she stood, one hand in her coat pocket clutching the card from the city boy, and with her other hand she waved again and again, calling, "Good-bye!"

Slowly the train started to move. Amory was yelling behind her, "We'll be back for Christmas!" At the same time Lucy felt him put his arm protectively around her for a moment before he went in.

Staying by the train door, she watched Mother and Father and the baby carriage disappear from sight. The train picked up speed and was soon past the cluster of low roofs that was her village of Wales. Finally at the south crossing, she had her last glimpse of her own road that Father had nicknamed The Edge of Nowhere.

"Good-bye, good-bye," she murmured under her breath. Then she turned around and entered the coach to join Amory and begin the long journey away from home.